When we were growing up, Rise had always been taller than me and I had to look up to him. Then last year I saw that I had caught up with him and could look him right in the eye. I stood next to him and he saw what was going on, but just sniffed at me and said I didn't smell like a real man. We laughed about that, and I liked when he kidded me.

Now I was getting the feeling that when Rise was saying one thing, there was something else going on behind the words.

Also by Walter Dean Myers

Fiction

Crystal

The Dream Bearer

Handbook for Boys: A Novel

It Ain't All for Nothin'

Monster
Michael L. Printz Award
Coretta Scott King Author Honor Book
National Book Award Finalist

The Mouse Rap

Patrol: An American Soldier in Vietnam
Jane Addams Children's Book Award

The Righteous Revenge of Artemis Bonner

Scorpions
Newbery Honor Book

Shooter

The Story of the Three Kingdoms

Street Love

Nonfiction

Bad Boy: A Memoir

Brown Angels: An Album of Pictures and Verse

I've Seen the Promised Land: The Life of Dr. Martin Luther King, Jr.

Malcolm X: A Fire Burning Brightly

Now Is Your Time!: The African-American Struggle for Freedom
Coretta Scott King Author Award

The Harlem Hellfighters: When Pride Met Courage

Awards

ALA Margaret A. Edwards Award

for lifetime achievement in writing for young adults

ALAN Award

for outstanding contribution to the field of young adult literature

WALTER DEAN MYERS

AUTOBIOGRAPHY OF MY DEAD BROTHER

ART BY CHRISTOPHER MYERS

Amistad

HarperTempest

An Imprint of HarperCollinsPublishers

Special thanks to Patrick Delisser, Reggie Forbes,
Jennifer Lewis and especially Abbas Hamad.
–C.M.

HarperTempest is an imprint of
HarperCollins Publishers.

www.harperteen.com
Library of Congress Cataloging-in-Publication Data
Myers, Walter Dean.
    Autobiography of my dead brother / by Walter Dean Myers ;
art by Christopher Myers.—1st ed.
        p.   cm.
    Summary: Jesse uses his sketchbook and comic strips to
make sense of his home in Harlem and the loss of a close
friendship.
    ISBN-10: 0-06-058293-6 (pbk.)
    ISBN-13: 978-0-06-058293-7 (pbk.)
    [1. Gangs—Fiction. 2. Friendship—Fiction. 3. Drive-by
shootings—Fiction. 4. African Americans—Fiction.]
I. Christoper Myers, ill. II. Title.
PZ7.M992Au 2005   2004027878
[Fic]—dc 22   CIP
                                                         AC
Typography by R. Hult
❖
First paperback edition, 2006

10 11 12 13 CG/RRDH 10 9 8 7

AUTOBIOGRAPHY OF MY DEAD BROTHER

Precious Lord, take my hand
Lead me on, let me stand
Lord, I am so tired
Yes, I'm weak
And yes, I'm worn . . .

"Lord knows we are tired today as we gather here in fellowship and sorrow, in brotherhood and despair, for the going-home ceremony of fourteen-year-old Bobby Green." Pastor Loving rocked forward as he spoke. "Lord knows we are tired of burying our young men, of driving behind hearses and seeing the painted letters of remembrance on the walls of our neighborhoods.

"As we close this chapter of young Bobby's life, let us send our prayers with him to the other side." Pastor Loving, a big, dark man, wiped the sweat from his forehead with his handkerchief. "Let us send our prayers with him so that maybe one day those left behind will finally be able to do what we hope for him—to rest in peace without the violence that blows through our community like the winds of winter. This loss chills the heart and challenges the soul, and yet we must keep on. To young Bobby's parents I extend my hand and the promise of a just God who will heal the heavy heart and rest the weary soul. As you leave the church today, stop and pass a word to Bobby's grieving mother, Louise, and his grieving father, John. Let them know that in the middle of darkness there is and will always be the everlasting light of Christian faith. Amen."

The gospel choir started singing softly, and row by row they left their seats. Bobby's mother was crying and leaning against an older man I didn't know. It was all the same, the gentle whirring of the fans, the familiar scent of the flowers, the hymns that filled the spaces between the people mourning Bobby. I looked over to where C.J. was still sitting at the organ. He looked small in front of the dark mahogany instrument. The people in the first row had started filing past the casket. My mom took my hand and squeezed it.

"I don't think . . ."

"It's okay," she said softly.

I slid out of the pew and made my way toward the back of St. Philip's Episcopal.

On the steps the cool evening breeze carried barbecue

smells from the Avenue. I watched as some young kids ran down the street to an ice-cream truck. It had been hot all day, and the few drops of rain that fell didn't cool things off at all.

"It's a shame for a child to go so young like that," Miss Essie Lassiter was saying. "It should have been somebody old, like me. Jesse, do the police have any idea who it was who shot him?"

"No, ma'am."

"That's the terrible thing about it," Miss Lassiter said. "First there's one shooting, and then there's a shooting getting even with that one, and people don't know when to stop."

"Yes, ma'am."

Bobby had a big family and they could afford only one official funeral car, so not too many people were going out to the cemetery. I watched as Miss Lassiter,

RUNNING
down the street

who went to everybody's funeral, got in one of the cars. A moment later they were pulling away from the church.

C.J. came up to me and he was looking teary-eyed. "You want to go over to the park?" he asked.

I said I'd go, and just then Rise came over. We told him where we were going and he said he'd come along. We walked the first part of the distance to the park in silence, and then Rise started kidding C.J. about not playing any jazz at Bobby G.'s funeral.

"You should have played like they used to down in New Orleans," Rise said. "Everybody would have talked about it."

"And my moms would have been all over my head," C.J. said. "I asked her about playing some jazz, but she said that Bobby's parents might not like it."

"Yeah, well, he went out like a man," Rise said.

"Yo, Rise, the brother got wasted in a drive-by," I said. "He was chilling on his stoop when some dudes lit up the sidewalk. I don't even think they knew who they shot."

We got to the park and sat on a bench. C.J. was talking about how Bobby was worried about getting into a good high school.

"We were just talking about that the other day," C.J. said. "He was saying that if he got into a good high school, he was going to bust his chops so he could go on to college. Bobby was cool."

"When your time comes, you got to go," Rise said. "That's all sad and everything, but that's the word, straight up."

"Maybe I should have played something special," C.J. said.

C.J. is the same age as me, fifteen. He was raised in the church and had been playing piano and organ for as long as I knew him. He wanted to play jazz, but his moms said he should stick to classical and gospel. We had talked about him sticking in a little jazz at Bobby's funeral, and I thought it would have been cool. I really didn't know Bobby's parents, though. Maybe they wouldn't have liked it. But there were so many funerals going on, it almost seemed you needed something to make them different.

"Y'all hear there's going to be a meeting of the Counts tomorrow?" Rise asked.

"For what?" C.J. had fished half of a candy bar from his pocket and was taking the paper off of it.

"It should be about Bobby G.," Rise said. "But Calvin is calling it, so I don't think it's going to be about anything, really. Dude is just swimming upstream and don't know where he's going."

On the far side of the park some guys had set up steel drums. They started playing some reggae, but real soft and it sounded good, almost like a pulse coming out of the darkness.

"You know, it's hard when somebody gets wasted,"

Rise went on. "Bobby G. was good people and everything, but that's why you have to make your life special every day. You never know when your time is up. Ain't no use in being down about it."

"I still wish I had played something special for Bobby," C.J. said. "It would have made me feel good, anyway."

An ambulance, its sirens wailing, sped past. My dad said that the main sounds in the neighborhood were sirens and gunshots. It really got him down.

"I got to get home," Rise said, standing up. "The meeting's at seven o'clock tomorrow. It better be short, too, because I'm not down for no all-night gabbing."

"See you tomorrow," I said.

Rise has this funny way of walking with one shoulder higher than the other one, and that made him look like he was bopping as he walked out of the park. We watched him get to the entrance and then turn and head down the hill toward Frederick Douglass Boulevard, where he lived.

"You know, maybe you can't tell when you're going to die," C.J. said, "but I still don't want to get shot for nothing in a drive-by."

"Guess what. I don't even want to be shot for something," I said. "When I go, I want the headlines to read 'Oldest man in the world died peacefully in his sleep with a smile on his face.'"

"And right under that it'll read, 'and his friend

RISE WALKS FUNNY

C.J. Europe played some jazz at his funeral.'"

We gave each other five and I smiled even though I noticed that C.J. had figured a way to live longer than me. The truth was, though, that Bobby's getting killed was scary. When we first heard about it, we were like all excited and everything, but when we got to the stoop and saw all the blood and the yellow police tape, it was still a shock. His mama was there crying and his cousin and soon everybody who knew him was messed around.

I didn't know exactly what it was. I didn't think that I was going to get shot in a drive-by or anything like that, but inside I was still nervous. I felt jumpy, not just when a strange car drove by, or some guys I didn't know were on the block, but all the time—even when I was in my kitchen having breakfast or in the supermarket or at home in bed. It was a drag, and I didn't want to talk to anybody about it.

"What are you eating?" I asked Dad.

"Watch your mouth, boy."

"I just want to know what you're eating," I said.

I knew what he was eating—two soft-boiled eggs and a small bowl of cereal. That's what the doctor had put him on and what he had said he would never eat again just the day before. I sat down at the table and looked over at his plate. I knew he wanted some bacon and fried eggs, but he was on a strict diet to get his weight down, and Moms was making him stick to it.

"You want to go bowling tonight?" he asked.

"Bowling? Do you bowl?"

"I guess I do," Dad said, as Mom came into the room.

"The doctor tell you that you had to get more exercise?" I asked. "'Cause I never saw you go bowling before."

"Your father's trying to sneak in some quality time with his son without mentioning that he's trying to sneak in some quality time with his son," Mom said.

"Girl, why do you have to run your mouth so much?" Dad asked.

"Because I think that you working on getting along with your son is a good thing and nothing you have to ease into as if you're ashamed of it, Mr. Givens," Mom said. "With the way this community is losing its way, we all need to do a little soul-searching and a lot of praying."

"You want to go bowling or not?" Dad asked, raising his voice.

"The Counts are having a meeting tonight," I said.

"How's Rise doing?" Mom asked.

"He's doing okay," I said.

Mom got back on Dad's case about how he and I should just be more open with each other and hang out together. She got to liking what she was saying and working it up until it sounded like a commercial. She even got into us going on a fishing trip.

"What I want to catch a fish for?" Dad asked. "You know I don't like fish."

"It's not about fishing," Mom said. "It's about the bonding."

"You got to use worms to catch a bond?" Dad asked, winking at me. "And how you cook it? Because if you can fry it up in some lard, maybe I'll go for it."

Mom flicked the tea towel at him and started putting the dishes into the sink while she checked the clock over the refrigerator.

Dad and Mom went to work together every morning. I got Mom's usual kiss on the forehead and a handshake from Dad that made Mom smile.

I knew the bonding thing was all about Bobby G. being killed. Mom was getting upset about so many kids getting shot and had already mentioned that maybe we should move out to the burbs. She worried a lot about me, and about Rise, too.

When we had first moved to 147th Street and Mom was looking for a babysitter so she could go to work, she had seen a sign on the church bulletin board that Rise's mother was taking care of kids. I was just one at the time, and Rise was almost three. His mother likes to tell the story that when Rise first saw me, he was scared of me. She said they had a puppy and a turtle and he liked to play with both of them, but when he saw me he started crying.

"The boy cried for the first two weeks I was keeping you," Mrs. Davis said.

I didn't remember any of that, but me and Rise grew up to be really close. He was more than my best friend— he was really like a brother. So when we saw an old movie on television about these two guys cutting themselves and mixing their blood to become blood brothers, we thought it was a good idea.

Rise was nine at the time and I was only seven, so it took a while to get up the nerve to cut myself. When I saw him bleeding, I chickened out and ran into the closet. Rise said I had to come out fast before the blood dried, but I was too scared. We had given up the idea, but then almost two weeks later I fell off the back of an over-stuffed chair that I had been riding as if it were a horse and scraped my arm really badly. I was screaming in pain and Rise was yelling something and went into the kitchen and got a knife.

He made a small gash on his finger and then put it against my scraped arm, and that's how we became blood brothers. His grandmother, who everybody called

Aunt Celia, saw us both bleeding and took us to the hospital. A nurse sprayed us with something that stung a little and sent us home.

When I was small I liked Rise's house better than mine, because Aunt Celia and his mother were always home and ready to make a snack or go to the park. His father wasn't there, and he hardly ever talked about him except to say he didn't care. I remembered once saying to Mom that I wished Dad would die so that I would have the same kind of family that Rise had. Mom said I'd get it straight after a while, and I did.

My parents both worked, but when they were home they were easy to be with. Mom kind of ran things, and me and Dad were her guys. There was a time when Rise would stay overnight at my house at least once a week, and I knew he liked it when he did. He doesn't stay over anymore and I can understand that, too. There are things you just don't do after a while.

Both of us had stopped collecting comic books, which we used to do big-time. When I was in the fifth grade we had gone to a comic book fair downtown and heard a collector say that the ideal number of comics to get was a thousand. You got a thousand and then you kept trading up, so that you got better and better comics instead of more and more.

Then one day Aunt Celia, who was getting strange, threw away a lot of Rise's comics. He was pissed. He said he wouldn't collect anymore and that it was a stupid thing to do, anyway. That made me feel bad, but I let it ride. It was just about then that we found out that Aunt Celia had Alzheimer's disease.

By that time I had begun drawing comics as well as collecting them. I liked to draw, and I could duplicate most of the superheroes pretty closely, some from memory. The superheroes I invented weren't great, but I was still working on the idea of getting my completely own comic book together.

Rise was like a brother to me, and also like my hero. Nobody messed with me, because they knew if they got up in my face, they would have to deal with Rise. He was smart in a deep way—not like school smart, when you know a lot of facts, but like the kind of smarts old people have. Even when I wasn't sure he was right, I listened to him carefully. We used to have long talks on his fire escape sometimes—just rapping about what was going on in the neighborhood or with our homeys. When Rise got into his junior year and got hooked up into taking SATs and thinking about college, we didn't hang as much as we used to. Then he started getting into trouble in school. It wasn't a big thing, really, just missing too many days or sometimes not coming back after lunch.

Once I asked him what was going down with his leaving in the middle of the day. He said he had a lot of things on his mind. I figured when he wanted me to know what they were, he would tell me.

I don't know exactly how me and C.J. started hitting it. What I think happened was that since we went to the same church and his mom knew my mom, she told him to make friends with me. He played organ and piano for the church, and he was good because he could play all the regular gospel stuff, some pop stuff, and he could read music. He was a little nerdy, but I didn't mind that because he was always straight up. Whatever C.J. was thinking he would say. He heard about the Counts and asked me to get him into the club. Since there weren't any rules about who got in and who didn't, it wasn't a big thing when he just started showing up at the meetings.

Me and Rise were friends because we had done a lot of things together and we liked each other. Me and C.J. weren't really all that tight, but we were cool with each other.

Back in the day, before there were Bloods, Crips, and other gangs, there were a lot of black social clubs. I got this from Calvin's father, who said he had belonged to three different clubs. The Counts, the one he was trying to keep going, was supposed to be over forty years old. Even my dad didn't remember it being around that long. But Mr. Reese, Calvin's father, had a picture of himself and three other guys in powder-blue tuxedos and bushy Afros that was signed on the back with "The Counts" written under the signature. I guess they were supposed to be funky or something.

Calvin's father wanted the club to live on and said that it needed some young people to carry on the traditions. Nobody was exactly sure what the traditions were, but it sounded like fun. We were meeting about once a month at different people's houses until Mr. Reese got us a room in the armory. He gave us a long talk about how we had to respect the armory and whatnot, and it was all good to the max. We got a television and a small refrigerator for the room, which really wasn't that big, and it was comfortable. At least it was good until Mason joined the Counts.

Mason Grier is seventeen, a year older than Calvin and two years older than me and C.J. The dude is definitely on a 24-7 hostility tour. The way he sees things is that there's him and there's the rest of the world. He's being righteous and the rest of the world spends all day trying to mess with him. When he heard about the Counts and wanted to get in, we said okay, because there weren't any real rules or anything, but nobody was digging him too tough.

Mason didn't do anything I could tell but hang around the block, but like one of the old West Indian dudes said after he and Mason got into an argument—he just felt like trouble.

That was true. When we heard he had been picked up for robbing a bodega on Lenox Avenue, two blocks up from the Schomburg, it was news but it wasn't a surprise.

"So this is what's going down," Calvin said, after calling the meeting of the Counts together. "We've got to talk about dues, about Mason, who you all know is in the slam, and about taking in a new member."

Calvin, Benny, Gun, me, and C.J. were at the meeting, and Benny reminded Calvin that we didn't have any dues. Calvin said he knew and that maybe it was time for us to start collecting a dollar a week dues just so we would have some backup cash. Everybody thought that was all right, so we had a vote and it passed 5–0. Then Rise showed and we had a new vote and it passed 6–0.

"Let's deal with the new man next," Calvin said. "He's outside, and I'll call him in and we can make a decision."

"We need to get some women into the club," Benny said. "Somebody call up the army and see how they recruit their chicks."

We had a quick vote on that and appointed C.J. to make the call. Then Calvin went out and got the new kid. Calvin explained that "Mr. Montgomery," as he called him, was applying for membership in the Counts.

"How old are you?" Benny asked.

"Old enough to get down." Mr. Montgomery looked like he could have been in the fifth or sixth grade.

"Lay some numbers on us." Rise eased into a chair.

"Fifteen," Mr. Montgomery said.

"What they call you?" Gun asked. "Baby Face Nelson?"

"My friends call me Little Man" was the quick answer. "Ain't nobody else supposed to speak to me."

The kid was showing hard, but nobody was down with it and you could tell.

"We'll let you know," Calvin said. "Give me a call sometime next week."

"That ain't good enough," Little Man said.

"Yeah, it is," Rise said. He got up and opened the door. "Now pretend your butt is a sail, and get on in the wind."

Everybody cracked on that, but I could tell that Little Man didn't go for it. He turned and gave each of us a dirty look and then tried to glide out the door, but Rise gave him a push and slammed the door behind him.

"We need a rules committee to figure out who we're taking in this club," he said. "They got to be at least weaned from their mamas."

We talked some more about collecting dues, and Rise said it was okay but maybe we should give a dance or something and try to raise some stash with some flash. That was all good, too, and we voted to collect a one-time dues payment of ten dollars and then plan a jump-and-bump to raise some more.

"We could have a dance and a ball game," Gun said.

"Yo, check it out!" Benny Gonzalez put his hands in his lap the way Gun does all the time. "We can have a dance *and* a ball game. If Gun ever gets married he's going to want to have a wedding—"

"*And* a ball game." Calvin finished Benny's sentence.

It was true. Gun could play some ball, and that's all he wanted to do. He was so serious about playing ball, he even studied to make sure he got into college so he could play on the next level. Plus the dude had made the All-City Team and the All-State Team, and was MVP in the

OUT THE DOOR

Catholic Midnight League.

"There's nothing wrong with basketball," Gun said, sounding kind of hurt.

"Gun, I'm thinking of taking you on in some one-on-one," C.J. said, leaning forward and drawling his words like he had something going on.

"C.J., if I wasn't so good to black people, I wouldn't even let you *say* basketball, let alone get your slow self on the court," Gun said.

"You mean C.J. can't hoop?" Benny asked. "I thought my man was an all-star."

"All-star?" Gun shook his head slowly. "I played C.J. some ball one day, and we couldn't finish the game because he played so bad, the ball got embarrassed and left."

I looked at C.J. and he was smiling.

"On a serious tip"—Calvin held his hand up—"there was one thing more that Mason asked me about."

"He's out of jail?" Rise asked.

"No, but his trial is coming up soon," Calvin said. "He told me that he wants the Counts to rough up the bodega store owner. Send him a message."

"He wants what?" Benny put his soda down. "And what did you say behind that?"

"The only witness against him is the store owner," Calvin said. "He said that if we went over and pushed him, you know, scared him, he probably wouldn't testify."

"Yo, man, that is so not together," Benny said. "The

dude's in jail and looking for company. He ain't getting my mama's child for a roommate."

"He said he didn't do it," Calvin said. "He said the Man is jacking him up and the store owner is going along with it."

"I'm not messing with it," Benny said. "You can bet on that."

"I didn't even hear what you said," Gun said.

"I got to decide." Rise had draped his sweater over a box and now picked it up and started putting it on. "Maybe we should be the no-Counts instead of the Counts. I don't know, if we're not willing to stand up for each other, maybe we should forget about the rest of the thing and just move on in our separate ways. No big thing. Eventually you reach manhood, then you got to go through or turn around and go back."

"This isn't about manhood," C.J. said. "This is about crime."

"Oh? Is Mason guilty?" Rise asked. "You know that? Or you just figure if a black man is arrested, he's automatically guilty?"

"Suppose he is guilty?" Gun asked.

"If it gets down to the word of the store owner against Mason, are they going to find him guilty?" Rise asked.

"Probably," C.J. said. "If he says that Mason was the one who stuck him up."

"So you're thinking about going along with him?" Calvin asked.

"Like I said, I got to decide," Rise said. "Same as you guys got to decide just how scared you are."

We were quiet as Rise left. I felt my heart beating a little faster as I tried to wrap my mind around what Rise had just said.

"Jesse, Rise is your dog, man," Calvin said. "Is he tripping?"

"I don't know, man," I said.

"I thought you were tight with him," Calvin said.

"I thought so too," I said.

So I'm home chilling. Facedown on my bed with the door open listening to the television in the next room. I was listening to a cartoon channel and imagining what the images were when Rise called.

"Why don't you come over for a while?" he asked.

"What's up?" I asked.

"Nothing," he said. "Just thought we could hang for a while."

"Yeah, okay."

We only lived a few blocks apart, but I took my time to get over to his place. When I'm going to talk to somebody serious, I like to have practice conversations with myself first. The whole thing with him talking about dealing with Mason was weird. When I thought about it, I knew we had drifted apart some and I hadn't spoken to him about it. As I was walking down the block, I realized that I didn't even know how to talk about something like that.

"Look, man, this bodega thing is not cool." That's what I was going to say. And I needed to have a hip way of saying it so that I wouldn't just sound like I'm laming out.

Or maybe: "Look, man, you're biting Mason's style but he's in Iron City, you dig?"

Mom would have told me to not worry about how I sounded, just come on out and say it. That sounds good for a woman but that's not me.

The guy who takes care of Rise's building is always mopping the floor down with disinfectant. He says it keeps down the germs. Maybe it does, but it smells so bad in the summertime, you have to hold your nose going up the stairs. Which I did.

Rise's grandfather, brown-skinned and thin except for a very round potbelly, answered the door.

"Hey, Rise!" he called out. "There's a tall, ugly stranger at the door!"

"Hello, Mr. Johnson."

"Come on in here, Jesse," he said, standing to one side. "And tell me how things been on the other side of the world. You have been on the other side of the world, haven't you?"

"No, sir."

Rise came up, and Mr. Johnson—he was Rise's mother's father—asked him if he knew me. Rise said no and they pretended they were going to put me out for a while until Mrs. Johnson, Aunt Celia, came out of her bedroom. You had to be careful around her, because she didn't understand things too tough.

I said hello to Aunt Celia and she smiled. She has a truly beautiful smile that makes her whole face light up. Whatever light is in a room is just fine for her face. The way I figured it, she must have been a stone fox when she was young. Rise and I went into his room, which is fixed up like a den, and he told me he had a jam he wanted me to hear. He put it on and it didn't sound like much to me.

"That's Coltrane," he said. "You ever hear of him?"

"I think so," I answered. "I didn't know you liked that kind of jazz."

"I'm moving on," Rise said, turning the music down. "Dealing with new sets, new issues."

"Like what?"

"Like what's coming down the street," Rise said. "What did Pastor Loving say? 'When I was a child, I thought as a child; but when I became a man, I put away childish things.'"

"Whatever."

I didn't like getting into the I'm-older-than-you rap, so I just let it slide, figuring he was coming back to it anyway. We talked a bit about what was going on in the hood, and Rise was talking about how school should be useful when mostly it wasn't. I was as chill as I could be and thinking about what I wanted to say about the bodega bit when Mr. Johnson knocked on the door. He opened it soon as he knocked on it and stuck his head in. I noticed that his eyebrows were mostly gray.

"Sidney Rock is out here," Mr. Johnson said. "Says he wants to talk to you."

Me and Rise went out to the kitchen and saw Sidney sitting at the table.

Sidney Rock was a cop, but he was okay with everybody on both sides of the Ave. He had grown up on the same block where I lived and hung out there a lot of the time. Everybody knew he was a cop even though he was young and dressed like an OG. He kind of looked out for all the brothers that he knew and that were straight with him. He'd also bust you if he had to, but at least he did it with respect. I had never seen him pull a gun but I knew he had one.

"What can I do for you?" Rise asked.

"Yo, Rise, what's up?" Sidney asked.

"I'm all good," Rise said. "How you doing?"

"Pumping strong." Sidney touched his chest over his heart. "I thought I'd run some thoughts by you and my man Jesse here just to clear up a few things."

"Run it," Rise said.

"These boys in any trouble?" Mr. Johnson asked.

"No, sir," Sidney said. "They know me—I don't make trouble and I don't look for it."

"Y'all need anything, I'll be in the next room," Mr. Johnson said. "And let me tell you something, Mr. Pidney—"

"Sidney, sir. The name is Sidney."

"Uh-huh." Mr. Johnson had his serious look on. "I know your folks."

"Yes, sir, I know you do."

Mr. Johnson went into the other room, and Rise said we should go into his room, which we did.

"Coltrane! All right!" Sidney recognized the music right away.

"So what you want, man?" Rise asked. He sat on the end of the bed.

"*Bam!* Just like that? Yeah, okay," Sidney said. "The word on the street is that Mason is trying to put out a hit on the bodega store owner, Mr. Alvarez."

"What's that got to do with us?"

"Nothing at all," Sidney said, smiling. "'Cause none of you are that dumb. I was just letting you know what the word was."

"How many snitches you got in your jail, Mr. Police-man?"

"Too many, my brother," Sidney said. "We got too many snitches, too many nonsnitches, and way too many young brothers trying to figure out how they got there."

"We all trying to figure out where we are," Rise came back.

"Jesse, you weren't planning to go down to the bodega, were you?" Sidney asked.

"Not really," I said.

"Yeah, that's about all I had to say." Sidney had been leaning against the wall, and he straightened up. "Glad to see you young brothers listening to some classical music. You know, I think I'm getting too old for rap."

"Whatever," Rise said. "Whatever."

"Yeah, well, you know me," Sidney said. "Why don't you give me a call if things start getting too heavy out here."

Sidney left, and Rise started cracking on him, imitating the way he spoke and stuff. I asked him why he was laughing, and he asked me if I didn't think he was funny.

"Sidney?" I asked. "I think he's a righteous dude."

"That's what he wants you to think, and he's got your mind all wrapped up in his act," Rise said. "Anyway, I called you over here to tell you I'm not going for Mason's play, either. He's out there on his own and we're going to leave him out there."

"I can hear that. That's what Sidney was saying, more or less."

WRAPPED UP

"You ain't hearing what I'm hearing, Jesse." Rise put the palms of his hands together and brought his fingertips to his lips. It looked almost as if he was going to pray or something. "What I'm hearing is that Mason thought he was a big man because he could run into the bodega and do his little number. But that's exactly what it's all about—a little number. The only real getover in the world is to be bigger than life. You know what I mean?"

"Like a superhero?"

"You've probably got the best brain on the block, man," Rise said. "Maybe I'll hire you to do my biography. You can start with a portrait of me and then write about what you see in it, like that nun on television. You can see my strength right in the picture. You hear what I'm saying?"

"I guess so."

"Thing is, when these street dudes do their muscle hustle, they got to lose, because sooner or later they're going to run into something stronger than they are," Rise said. "Mason is sitting in Iron City trying to figure out how he's still being strong. He sees the lines, but he just don't get the picture. You know what I mean?"

"Yeah," I said.

What Rise was saying about Mason was heavy. I was sure I was seeing all the lines, too.

"So what makes you think Rise is different?" We were sitting in the church at the organ and C.J. was doodling over the keys.

"I guess it was more about how he was talking about being different," I said. "You know how he used to wear his hair long, but now he's into dreads and silver cord in his hair."

"Silver cords?"

"Braided into the dreads," I said. "It looks all right, but it's different."

"Maybe he's just getting old."

"I don't know," I said. "He's changed a lot in the last year or so. I used to know everything about him. We were real close."

"Rise probably thinks he has to act differently because he's taking over the Counts," C.J. said.

"He's not taking over the Counts," I said. "I mean, we're not like something you take over, anyway."

"That's not what he told Calvin. He told Calvin that from now on, Mason can't tell us what to do and if he sends any messages, he should send them to him. That sounds like taking over to me."

C.J.'s mama came from the church basement carrying a plate of something. She stopped and looked at me and asked how hungry I was.

"And I know you're hungry because it's the nature of boys to be hungry," she said.

"No, I'm okay," I said.

"What are you and C.J. up here plotting?" she asked, putting the plate of potato salad and sliced ham down in front of C.J. "I know it must be the Lord's work."

"C.J. was just sitting here working on some blues he was thinking about playing at service next Sunday," I said.

"Jesse Givens, how are you going to sit here in church and lie like that?" C.J. had this big grin on his face.

"Now one of you is lying," Mrs. Europe said. "And it doesn't matter if I know which one it is because God knows and He will deal with you gentlemen."

"You know it must be Jesse," C.J. said, "'cause I don't even like the blues."

"I was telling C.J. that the blues are the devil's music, Mrs. Europe," I said, "but I don't think he was listening."

"You know, there was a time when I sang the blues." C.J.'s mother put her head to one side. "I bet you didn't know that, did you?"

"No, ma'am."

"But then I got a regular job in the post office and gave up singing because it wasn't paying any money," she said. "And if I thought playing the blues could lead to a good job, I wouldn't mind C.J. playing them."

Right on cue C.J. started playing some blues on the organ and Mrs. Europe gave him a whack across the hands and reminded him that he was in church.

On the way home I was thinking about C.J. and how easy it was to hang out with him. He wasn't that easy a guy to know, because he never talked about himself. All he ever wanted to do was play his music and be left alone. But I liked him. When we were together, there was never any tension between us.

That used to be the way it was with me and Rise. We used to hang out at his house, especially when it rained, and just watch television all day. I always had more money than he did and we would go over to the super-market and buy some junk food to eat while we checked out the cartoons or sometimes the talk shows if they were stupid enough, and they usually were.

When we were growing up, Rise had always been taller than me and I had to look up to him. Then last year I saw that I had caught up with him and could look him right in the eye. I stood next to him and he saw what was going on, but just sniffed at me and said I still didn't smell like a real man. We laughed about

31

that, and I liked it when he kidded me.

Now I was getting the feeling that when Rise was saying one thing, there was something else going on behind the words. He was still talking to me, so I got the feeling that he was saying something that he wanted me to know. I didn't know why he didn't tell me that he was taking over the Counts.

I was easy with Sidney, too. He was a cop and everybody was supposed to be a little uptight with cops because we were all, like, deep down gangsters and just chill prowling to keep people out of our bizness, but Sidney was righteous. When he ran down the numbers about how Iron City had so many brothers hooked up that it looked like Homeyville, you had to pay some attention.

When I got home, the house was in an uproar. Mom was all upset and Dad had a towel around his foot. There was blood on the floor.

"What happened?"

"He cut his foot and he won't go to the hospital!" Mom said. "I wish we had a police dog here to bite his butt."

"How did your foot get cut?" I asked.

"It's nothing," Dad said. "Your mama's just panicking over nothing."

"The fool had an ingrown toenail and cut his foot trying to cut the nail," Mom said. "I hope it gets infected and falls off!"

There was a blood trail that led from the doorway to Dad's chair. It looked serious. "Why don't you go to the hospital and get it taken care of?" I asked.

"And have to answer a bunch of stupid questions about how I cut my foot?" Dad shook his head no.

One of the things I liked about my father was that it was only him and me who did stupid things around the house.

"When that foot is hurting about two o'clock in the morning, don't ask me to get up and get aspirins for you!" That from Mom.

"Can I see it?" I asked.

It didn't look that bad, but I thought it needed to be taken care of because it could get infected.

I thought about doing a cartoon of Dad with his foot all bandaged up. Sometimes when I did cartoons of my folks, it made them laugh. I thought a cartoon of Dad with his hurt foot would just get him madder, so I didn't bring it up.

I went to my room and took out my sketch pad,

thinking about C.J. asking me how Rise was different. I thought some more about Rise's new hairstyle. I did three quick sketches, trying to draw his hair, but none of them looked right. Then I set up my small easel and clamped a pad to it and thought I would draw Rise's face from memory and then the hair would come out naturally. I worked on it for a while, and then Mom knocked on the door.

"He's finally decided to go down to the emergency room to have his toe looked at," Mom said. She had her sweater on and her keys in her hand. "Can you believe that man?"

I just smiled and she started to go, saw the easel, and asked me if she could look.

"Go ahead."

Mom looked, and smiled approvingly. "That's a nice drawing," she said. "Who is it?"

After my folks left, I looked all over my room for pictures of Rise. I stuck them up with tape all around the drawing I had done.

I had done pictures of Rise before, and some good ones. Mom had bought me a little desk with drawers to keep my drawings and art supplies in, and I went through it until I found some of the old drawings. I found two good sketches of Rise and compared them to the photographs I had taken of him. The photographs were instant

prints in color, but none of them were as good as the sketches. Then I compared the sketches to the drawing I had done from memory. Mom was right—it didn't look like Rise or any of the photographs.

"Okay, so what we can do is to start a Cuban band," Benny was saying. "It's going to be me on sax, C.J. on box, Calvin on bass, and everybody else playing rhythm. We'll call ourselves the Exiles."

"We're not Cuban," Calvin said.

"So what? The Grateful Dead weren't dead, either," Benny said. "That's what you need, a name that's like completely made up so people know you're different."

"They're going to know I'm different when I can't speak Spanish," Calvin said.

"And what's Cuban music about, anyway?" I asked.

"It's about rhythm," Benny said. "This is a party for eleven- and twelve-year-old kids. All they want to do is to shake their little booties around and look good. We pull this off and we're going to get a hundred and fifty bucks. That's five of us, and we end up with thirty bucks apiece for two hours' work."

"I thought you said your two cousins are going to

play?" Calvin said. "Five and two is seven. That comes to twenty dollars and change apiece."

"That's still ten dollars an hour!" Benny said. "And say somebody hears us and we sound good. Then we get a record deal and it's getover time."

"We should have a movie of us playing on a big screen behind us," I said. "That way we can keep it reel and real."

"Whatever," Benny said. "You dudes in?"

"I'm in," I said.

"I'm not worried about you," Benny said. "C.J., you're the man. You in?"

I don't know how C.J. got his mouth to work like that, but he got it going and it came out with a yes.

Benny went on about how this could be our big break in life and how one day we were going to think back on our start. All the while I knew me and C.J. were thinking the same thing—how he was going to get this past his moms.

After Benny and Calvin left, I turned and looked at C.J. and he looked away. Near the curb a little girl was beating her doll and screaming at it, and I nudged C.J. for him to look. The girl was about eight and skinny. Her hair wasn't combed.

C.J. held out his fists as if he was holding a stick. "Crraaack!" he said.

"Her?"

"Her mama," C.J. said.

We watched the girl beat up on the doll awhile longer,

and it made me feel bad. When C.J. asked me if I wanted to take a walk down to the corner to get a soda, I said okay. We went down to the corner, past a small mountain of garbage bags that hadn't been picked up that morning and a trillion kids playing around them.

"My mother was thinking about moving," C.J. said. "Except she wants me to keep playing piano in the church, and she thinks that if I move away, I'll just keep finding excuses not to get over and play anymore."

"She right?"

"I want to play." C.J. played some air piano. "You know I love playing more than anything. And I love the way she sits on me to keep me out of trouble and everything."

"But you want to fly?"

"Fly? I just want to walk a little. Nothing wrong with playing in a Cuban band."

"Can you play Cuban music?"

"There's no Cuban music," C.J. said. "There's just music. If you can play, you can play. And if you can feel it, you can play it."

"I can feel it and I can't play," I said.

"That's because your brain is wired wrong," C.J.

wired

said as we went into the corner grocery. "Your brain is wired up for pictures like a kid's brain. I'm sophisticated, like Beethoven and Duke Ellington. You never heard of a sophisticated artist. All artists do is drink cheap wine, draw naked ladies with three eyes, and cut their ears off and stuff like that."

We got some sodas and C.J. bought some potato chips. Whenever he was nervous, he always ate too much, which is why he was heavy. That was one reason. The other was that his mother was always bringing him some food. She was like a mother bird always coming back to the nest with a worm or something and C.J. always had his mouth open.

"I did a picture of Rise and it came out all wrong," I said.

"You sweet on Rise?"

"Get out of here!" I pushed him through the door as we left. "Why you say something like that? He asked me to do it. He said I should write his biography."

"He wants his biography, he should write it," C.J. said. "He knows what he did."

"I know what he did too," I said. "I've been with him all his life, or at least most of it. The thing is he's been changing so much, and I'm looking at him and I'm seeing him, but somehow the picture I did of him isn't right and I've done good pictures of the guy. Some of the pictures I did just last year are really good ones. Even my

40

mother didn't recognize the picture of him I did the other day."

"Maybe you're past your prime." C.J. crumpled the empty bag of chips and dropped it in a garbage can.

"Yo, C.J., how did you finish those chips that fast? You just walked out of the store!"

"I got a feel for eating potato chips," C.J. said. "It's like a secret talent."

We got back to the stoop and the little girl was gone, but her doll was lying on the sidewalk, next to the fire hydrant.

C.J. was talking about how if we got a Cuban band together, we could really make some money. He said that all we needed was one good record contract and that we wouldn't spend all our money on bling-bling but buy some houses or something useful.

I was down with what he was saying, but all the time I was thinking about that doll lying on the sidewalk. It was beat-up and dirty, but I knew that at one time it was new and pretty and somebody had loved it. If I had a sketchbook with me, I would have drawn it.

Once I had started carrying a sketchbook around and drew things that I saw on the street, or people, or even some of the stores along the block. Then some older guys asked why I was drawing them and told me not to do it even when I said I wasn't drawing them. They took my sketchbook and tore it up right in front of me, which

made me feel bad. It wasn't about what I was drawing so much as it was about me having something I could do. It made me feel good knowing that too. I could draw, like C.J. could play his music. And when you have something you can do, you can always bet that somebody won't like it and try to take it away from you.

"So what you got to do"—C.J.'s voice broke through my thoughts—"is to tell your mama to call my mama and ask her if I can play in the Cuban band."

"Yeah, okay."

Saturday morning. It was the end of June and there were two months left before I would really have to start thinking about school again. Moms had said it would be all right for me to go down to Cooper Union and see about the art courses, but if I didn't get in she wanted me to find a job somewhere. I was down with me working, but Dad wasn't. What he said was that work didn't do you any good unless you needed the job or loved the job. The real deal was that he was always imagining something terrible was going to happen to me. Mom said he was like an old hen sitting on her last egg. I guess the last egg was me.

Anyway, it's Saturday morning and the phone rings and there's my mother's knock on my door.

"Yeah?"

Mom's head in the doorway. "Yeah? What kind of greeting is that in the morning?"

"Yes, sweet mother dear." I sat up in bed. "Sweetest

of the sweet and fairest of the fair. Queen of all that's good and noble."

"That's not bad," Mom said. "Keep working on it. Benny is on the phone."

I got to the phone and Benny asked me if I had heard the news, which ticked me off. I hate it when people ask you one question and that's not really what they want to say, but then you have to say something to get to the real thing.

"What news?"

"The bodega got firebombed last night," Benny said. "Nobody got hurt, but there's cops all around the place. Two white cops said they were looking for you."

"Get out of here," I said. "Ain't no police looking for me."

"That's what Dorothy Dodson told me," Benny said. "And she doesn't go around making stuff up. They said that yesterday a young-looking black guy went into the bodega with a gun and threatened the owner."

"And who figured out I'm the only young-looking black guy in Harlem?" I asked. "That's so lame it's pitiful."

"So you think Dorothy's making it up?"

I didn't think she was making it up, because that's not what she's about, but I didn't know why they were look-ing for me.

Pop must have heard me talking to Benny. When I

got off the phone, he asked what was going on, and I told him, and he asked me if he should contact Joe Charles, our family lawyer.

"For what?"

"I don't like messing around with the police," he said.

"I haven't done anything, so there's nothing to worry about," I said.

"So how are you going to find out what's going on?" Mom asked. She and Dad were standing in the doorway.

"You have any idea what this is about?" Dad asked.

"I heard Mason wanted to muscle up the guy in the bodega," I said.

"Mason? Who's that?" Dad grunted out the words.

"He was in the Counts for a while," I said. "Then he was arrested for holding up the bodega."

"The bodega that was firebombed?" Mom asked.

"Yeah."

"And how are you involved in it?"

"I'm not!" I said.

I went on about how they were making a big deal of the whole thing, but I wasn't sure. There was nothing for me to worry

FIREBOMBED

about, because I hadn't even been in the bodega and I wouldn't even know how to set it on fire.

My folks were real quiet and I could see they were worried. When I sat at the kitchen table and started dialing, Mom was washing dishes, very quietly, and Dad was reading Friday's paper, also very quietly.

"Hello, Mrs. Europe?"

"Hello, Jesse, what are you doing up so early?"

I looked at the clock on the wall and saw that it was five minutes to seven. "I didn't realize it was early, ma'am. I just wanted to speak to you for a minute."

"Speak to me or speak to C.J.?"

"Uh, you, I guess."

"Well, you got me," Mrs. Europe said.

"Some of us were thinking about starting a band to play over the summer," I said. "And the thing we're missing is a good piano player."

"Uh-huh." She could give out the flattest uh-huhs I had ever heard.

"And I was thinking that I knew that C.J. wouldn't want to play in a band that played Latino music, but maybe you could help to convince him that it would be all right because some really nice guys, like me, are going to be in the band. Ma'am."

"I thought your mother was supposed to call me and try to convince me," Mrs. Europe said.

"Oh."

C.J.'s mother laughed and asked to speak to my mother. I gave Mom the phone, telling her who it was. The whole time they were talking, and I could tell it was about the Cuban band, the expression on Mom's face was about what did it have to do with the bodega and about the police looking for me.

When Mom hung up, she asked me if there was anything she needed to know.

"And you know I'm not talking about playing in some band," she said.

"If you think I'm into setting fires in bodegas, then you don't have a clue to who I am," I said.

Dad put his paper down. "I didn't know anything about this Mason guy because you didn't tell me anything," he said. "I didn't know anything about this bodega stickup because you didn't tell me that, either."

"I didn't do it, so I didn't think it was that important," I said.

"It involves my son, it's important," Dad said. There was a catch in his voice, and I could see he was getting really emotional. "You got that? You got that, Jesse?"

"Yeah, I got it," I answered.

I hung around for a while, did some quick sketches of Rise, and then called C.J. and asked if he could meet me downstairs. I put on my sneakers and some shorts, then changed into some jeans and went down. C.J. was on the stoop with Bianca and Miss Essie. I asked him if he wanted to go over to see the bodega, and he said okay and got up.

"You don't say good morning to your elders, Jesse?" Miss Essie asked.

"Good morning, Miss Essie."

"Did that hurt your face?"

"No, ma'am."

On the way over to the bodega, C.J. said his mother was "thinking" about letting him play in the band. He said that was a good sign.

"What did your father say?"

"He'll go along with anything she says," C.J. said.

There was a small crowd on the corner where the bodega was. An emergency fire truck was parked down the street, and some guys in yellow slickers and fire helmets were standing outside the store drinking coffee. We got closer and saw that the whole store was burned black.

"Oh, man!" C.J. whistled through his teeth. "It looks like a bomb hit it."

"So what do you think?" The voice came from behind me and made me jump. I turned and saw Sidney standing a foot away from me.

"It's really something," I said, which sounded kind of stupid.

"I wonder if you would do me a favor," Sidney said. "I want you to come over to the Island with me and just tell Mason how it looks. Think you can do that?"

"Rikers Island?" I asked.

"I can do that," C.J. volunteered.

"No, not you," Sidney said. "I've already asked Rise and now I'm asking my man Jesse here. You don't mind, do you, Jesse?"

I heard my mouth saying "No, I don't mind." I hate when my mouth surprises me like that.

Sidney called my folks and had a talk with them to make sure it was all right for me to go. They said it would be all right, and late Monday night Rise and I were waiting for Sidney to pick us up on 125th Street and Lenox Avenue. It was raining, and the slight wind was enough to blow the cheap umbrellas inside out.

"How come we had to meet him down here?" I asked, pulling the collar of my jacket shut.

"Can't have people seeing me dealing with the Man," Rise said, slightly slurring his words. I knew he was fronting cool.

"My dad said there used to be a big clock on a jewelry store across the street," I said, getting away from Rise's Gollywood act.

"Yeah, yeah."

Rise looked up and down the street as if he was afraid somebody was watching us. It got me a little ticked, because I didn't want to deal with his attitude. I couldn't use his act so I just jammed my hands into my pockets and let it go.

For some reason I thought Sidney was going to ride up in a police car, but it was a private car. I sat in front and Rise slid in the backseat. Sidney asked if we needed anything to eat, and Rise said no before I had a chance to say anything.

We drove over the Triborough Bridge, and Sidney asked me how often I went to Queens.

"I go to Shea Stadium sometimes," I said. "When they give out free tickets down at the YMCA."

"Yeah, that Y is okay," Sidney said. "Back in the day they used to have political meetings there and everything. That's where I got recruited for the police department. I was only nineteen."

That made sense, because the police were right down the street from the Y. I didn't know how old Sidney was, but I figured he was twenty-something because he looked young.

The streets of Queens are darker than the ones in Manhattan and we couldn't see much. Sidney told us we weren't actually going to Rikers, which was a jail, but to a place the city ran so that some nonviolent inmates could serve part of their sentence as close to the World as possible.

"So that's where Mason is doing his gig?" Rise asked.

"No, that's just where the meeting is going to be

held." Sidney glanced up at Rise in the rearview mirror. "Armed robbery is not about nonviolence."

We drove in silence for a while, and then Sidney pulled the car over in front of a small brick building. It looked more like a factory than where somebody lived. He cut the engine and then turned halfway around in his seat so he could see both of us.

"You guys are friends of Mason's," he said. "I thought you might talk to him about the difference between armed robbery and homicide. You know what the difference is?"

"Armed robbery is when you stick somebody up," I said. "And homicide is when you kill somebody."

"What you think, Rise?"

"I think Jesse got it," Rise said, still being cool.

"The thing is," Sidney said, "that it's not so different on the 'doing' side. You walk in with a gun and you're thinking about armed robbery and the getaway. Then something happens—your buzz gets freaky or the guy you're trying to take off gets jumpy—and you move your finger a half inch and somebody's dead. Not much difference there. A half inch, a second one way or the other, a twitch.

"But on the other side, the results side, there's a big difference. All of a sudden there's somebody lying on the ground with his life oozing away. And when you get caught, you're facing twenty-five years to life in New

York. That means you're gone for twenty years if you behave yourself. And guess what—you don't recover those years. You don't come back and start all over. You're twenty years behind the rest of the world, and the world's not going to let you forget it."

"If you get caught," Rise said.

"Like Mason." Sidney smiled. "Like Mason. So maybe you can tell him the difference so he can pull back from doing anything more to that bodega owner."

"You think he was the one who got the place fire-bombed?" I asked.

"I don't know for sure," Sidney said. "But I do know that seven to ten for armed robbery gives you a chance. You get twenty years and the plate's empty. You know what I mean?"

"I guess so," I said.

Sidney didn't wait for Rise to answer. We got out of the car, and he rang the bell in front of the house. The man who answered the door was heavy, with a big, sad-looking face that almost smiled when Sidney introduced us as his friends.

We were taken to a room that had a couch against one wall and two overstuffed chairs on the side walls. There were lamps on the end tables near the couch. On the far wall, next to a door, was a television. The wire was on top of it. There was one window. It was slightly open, and the light-green curtains moved away from the bars when the wind blew. Sidney told us to have a seat and relax.

"All that talk was supposed to be for us," Rise said when Sidney had left. "We were supposed to be like all impressed and everything about how scary the slam was and how everybody was going to get caught. He looks like a brother and tries to sound like one, but he's still the Man. You can put in my book that when the Man was dealing lies, I was real-a-lizing what he was trying to put down. You got that?"

"Yeah, I got it." I thought Sidney was okay, but I didn't want to deal with Rise.

We sat there for a while and I was getting a little nervous. Maybe Rise was right, that if the guys on the block knew me and him were dealing with Sidney, it could be a problem that they wouldn't trust us anymore. One of the things about the hood was that there was this anxious bit with the cops. Everybody knew we had to have cops around so the thugees wouldn't rule, but we had to be all like "don't be in my face with it" at the same time.

But Rise's play had got to me. He was like slipping into this whole role thing and I didn't know how to handle it. Sidney was trying to do Mason a solid, and Rise was dealing as if it was all some kind of trick bag. It came to me that maybe what Rise was doing was putting marks in the air, the way I did on paper, trying to do a self-portrait that I would believe and copy. What I was thinking, not deep but bubbling along the surface of my mind, was that when I put my marks down on paper, lines and shades and figures, I was looking for what was the truth behind the real thought he was keeping. That's what I was thinking at the same time I was thinking that writing and drawing was what I did and I wanted to get to it even if it was on the back of Rise's wagon. At least that's what I was thinking until the door opened and Mason came in.

MAKING MARKS

Mason was limping as he came through the door. He went quickly to one of the single chairs, barely glancing at Rise and me. He picked up a magazine on the arm of the chair and started thumbing through it, pretending to ignore us. Rise plugged in the television and clicked it on with the remote.

It was late Monday, and the sports channel Rise had turned on was going over the day's baseball games. There was a clock on the wall over the set, and I could see the sweep hand move over the face of the clock in slow motion. I hadn't been nervous before Mason came in, but as soon as he sat down I started having trouble breathing.

He was in street clothes and perped down, with his pants hanging low on his hips and his sneakers open.

"So I see you keepin' on," Rise said, pulling at his crotch.

"See you and Jesse out here pimping for the Man," Mason said. "What he tell you to say? Because I know that's all you got in your heads."

"Nobody tells me what to say." Rise rolled his eyes toward Mason and hunched his shoulders forward. "Nobody tells me nothing!"

"Yeah, Calvin said you trying to bark like a big dog." Mason closed the magazine. "But you still come in here with your tail between your legs and sniffing on that cop's hind parts."

"You hear about the bodega being firebombed?" I asked. I heard my voice shoot up and gulped while I tried to calm it down. "It was really messed up."

"Yeah, I heard it. That's why they bring you in here? To see if I ordered it?"

"What you going to order from Iron City?" Rise asked. "Somebody did you a favor and you don't even appreciate it. That's what I think."

"That's all you supposed to think, chump."

"Chump? You the one eating boiled hot dogs and scrambled eggs. I'm the one going home tonight," Rise said.

"You got a lawyer?" I asked.

"Kelly. Black dude acting like he wish he was white."

Mason picked up the magazine again. "I ought to represent myself."

"So you could just walk out now?" I asked.

"Naw, man. They got dogs and locks on everything. You ain't walking from here. That's what they want me to do. You know, cop a sprint so they come after me and light me up. They ain't letting me out. I'm too dangerous, man. They get me on the street, they don't know what's going to happen. That's the whole thing right there. They want some chumps they can control."

The Red Sox were on the screen, and there was a fight after the pitcher hit some guy with a pitch in the back of his legs. We watched the fight awhile and I began to realize I was freaking out a little. I didn't like being in the room.

"S-S-Sidney said—" I was stuttering. "Sidney said that if you did order the firebombing you ought to cool it, because if somebody died you would get homicide."

"They can give you anything they want to give you," Mason said. He hunched forward, and his shoulders shook a little before he went on. "They got everything on their side. They want to plant some evidence on you, they do it. They got the power in here, and they jacking up people on the street."

"You got your manhood and that's all you need." Rise stretched his legs out in front of him and crossed them at the ankles.

"What you know about anything?" Mason asked. "All you know is what you heard. I'm out here in the war. You see this place? This ain't about what you seen on TV. This is the Big Keep."

"Still doesn't make any sense bombing the bodega and risking twenty years in jail," I said, trying to calm things down.

"Not when the dudes who are supposed to be watching my back are running with the Man," Mason said. "I sent out a message for the Counts to talk to the bodega dude, and all I got back is static. What's that about?"

"You in the slam and we're in the World," Rise said. "You don't send out no messages, you send out *requests*. You know what a request is?"

"Yeah, I'm hip to what you're saying." Mason stood up, and Rise stood up to face him. "What you saying is that you're Superman. Ain't that right? Faster than a speeding bullet. Leaping tall buildings and whatnot. Ain't that right? Ain't your black butt faster than a speeding bullet, Rise?"

"I take care of myself," Rise said. His voice sounded less sure.

Mason took a step toward him and then another until they were no more than inches apart. I could see Rise's chest move as he breathed. It seemed right to say something, but my throat was dry.

Mason leaned close so that his mouth was next to

THE BIG KEEP

Rise's ear. When he spoke it was like a whisper, raspy and low. And scary.

"I ain't got nothing to lose, man. They got me in here, and anything they want to do with me, they can swing it. Anything they want to pin on me, they can do that, too," he said. "But the Counts are my peeps, and if you think you stepping into my shoes, you wrong. You just think about what you're hearing tonight. When you thinking about standing up against me, just remember that the only one of us that got something to lose is you because I don't care about a thing. Life don't mean nothing to me."

Mason turned slow and walked to the door he came in. He didn't say "so long" or anything, just left.

Rise said something. The last part of the sentence was "out of here" and he started to leave. My legs felt weak, and I sat down and took a deep breath. I asked him to wait a minute and he did.

"You okay?" he asked.

"Yeah."

When we were going past the police sitting at desks in the next room, I noticed that Rise was shaky too.

In the car headed back to Harlem, we were all quiet. Sidney said he knew a place where we could get some burgers and drinks, but me and Rise both said no.

"We could eat them in the car if you don't want to be seen with the Man," Sidney said, smiling.

"I'm okay," I said.

Rise didn't say anything.

We dropped Rise off on 125th Street, and I said okay when Sidney asked if I wanted him to take me up to my block.

"What do you think of Mason?" Sidney asked me as he parked the car.

"He's different," I said. "He's like a different kind of guy."

Sidney looked at me. "That's maybe the best description I've heard of people like him," he said. "He is a different kind of person. It's as if there's a line out there someplace, and people like him cross it, and we don't know them anymore."

"I guess."

I went upstairs and my mom was on the phone. Sidney had called on his cell phone and told her I was coming up. I said I was tired and going to bed, and she asked me if I had had a good evening.

"It was okay," I said.

Rise called before I fell asleep.

"I might get you to make me a cape," he said. "Maybe I am Superman. Might as well be, huh?"

I said I guessed so, just to get him off the phone. I lay in bed for a long time thinking about seeing Mason and watching him and Rise push up on each other. What I realized was that I didn't know what was going on with them.

I spent three afternoons drawing on some old comic-book paper I had bought on Canal Street. The paper was a little curled on the edges, but I taped it to my drawing board and put in the boxes that I wanted. The thing to do was to put the boxes in and then draw the comics so that they came out of the boxes whenever I wanted them to look more dynamic.

I did them all in pencil and then inked a few of them just to show Rise what they would look like. They came out really good, and I was glad I had done three complete pages before taking them over to him.

"What's this scene?" he asked.

His grandmother was sitting at the head of the table, smiling. She didn't remember who I was anymore, and I felt sorry for her, but she spooked me out a little with her smile.

"You remember that birthday party you had and somebody hung up a piñata?" I asked. "And your father came over?"

MRS. JOHNSON

"Yeah, and he picked you up and he didn't pick me up," Rise said.

"What?"

"I remember that party. That was, like, my first real party. I was all excited and everything because Pops came over. I see you didn't put him in," Rise said. "That's good, because that's the way I felt, too. No, maybe I didn't feel that way then, but later . . . you know."

"Yeah," I said, not really knowing what he was talking about. "Then here was where we used to go downtown to Morningside Park. You remember that?"

"Now that you got it all drawn up I do." Rise straightened the paper. "All that stuff is somewhere in my head, but I can't bring it up the way you do. How you remember all this stuff, man?"

"So I think I'll clean the living room," his grandmother said.

"No, that's all right, Grandma." Rise patted his grandmother's folded hands. "It looks good from when you cleaned it this morning."

"Dr. Craft loves a clean living room," she said, still smiling.

She got up and took the bottle of dishwashing liquid off the sink and headed toward the living room. Rise went to the door and called his grandfather. He said that his grandmother was cleaning the living room again.

Then he came back to the kitchen and started looking over my drawings again.

"You got to put in us becoming blood brothers," he said. "But make the knife real big."

"Dramatic."

Big Knife

"Yeah, yeah. This is all tight. You got that art thing going on good."

"Your grandmother going to be okay?"

"I guess so," Rise said. "I'm going to be looking for my own place soon. Then when I move they can set up a little place for her to sit in the daytime. She's always talking about fixing up a regular parlor or something."

"You got the money to pay rent?"

"Money ain't no big thing." Rise inhaled deeply through his nose. "I been talking to some people about some business. Maybe even get the Counts in on the action. I haven't got it all figured out yet."

"What kind of business?"

"I don't want to lay it out cold," Rise said, still looking at the drawings. "You going to finish these? Put color on them and whatnot?"

"First, I'm going to do them over in pencil, then decide which ones I want to keep," I said. "Then when I finish the whole layout—"

"Then you tighten it up with color and shading."

"Right."

"Yeah, I can dig that. That's me and you playing in front of your house and that's Moms—what's she doing?—calling me—no! That's when that dude was driving backward down the street!"

"I knew you would remember that," I said.

"And Moms was standing there screaming and you

and me almost got wasted. If that dude hadn't hit that light pole, he would have messed up about eight or nine of us."

"At least," I said.

"This means a lot to me," Rise said, "these pictures."

He said he was moving on, sliding up the scale, and having some ink on his days was hip. "It's like the Man said, if you ain't in the book, you come and you go and you ain't never been."

"How are you going to get a place of your own?" I asked. "You going to leave school and get a job?"

"Look, Jesse, strictly between you and me, I got the word from some people uptown that they need a new wheel to deal the downtown blow," he said. "They want to hook up with the Counts, but you know, I don't know if the Counts are ready to deal on that level. I got to do what you're doing, draw it all up in my head and see what I want to keep. Figure out what's real and what I need to let burn. You know what I mean?"

"Yo, you got to be jiving, right?" I asked. "That doesn't even sound like you. All the time you talking about not doing drugs and how that stuff is sucking the life out of the hood, and now you're radioing about dealing? What kind of crap is that?"

"That's what I'm talking about," he said. "You're not down with it, and I know Benny's paranoid. Little Man saw me on the street the other day, and he was asking where he could cop a piece so I figure he's in the street."

"Little Man's a kid," I said. "I thought you didn't even want him in the Counts."

"I didn't say I did," Rise said. "All I'm saying is that I'm putting everything together, the same way you are with your little drawings, and figuring what I'm going to keep and what I'm going to throw away."

"Where do you think dealing is going to carry you?" I asked.

"Yo, I guess I don't know, Reverend Givens. Let me see. Let me see. Could it be down the road to hell and damnation? How about the fast lane to wrack and ruin? How about the easy way to get my picture done in chalk? Maybe you could tell the Man to let you slip under the tape and do the picture right. What you say, Reverend?"

"Nothing you don't know," I said.

"Look, Jesse, let me tell you what the deal be," Rise said. "Everybody knows there are things out there that are righteous and things you need to leave alone, right?"

Do the picture right

"Go on."

"And some people are going to pick up the bad stuff and somebody is going to supply it, right?"

"I've heard this before," I said.

"So does that mean it's not true?" Rise asked. "Does it mean that it's true but you can't deal with it? Or does it just mean you want to close the book on me?"

"All it means it that I'm, like, falling apart inside. I can't figure out where all this is coming from. One day we're talking the same talk and the next day it's Greek and Russian, and I don't understand squat."

"Yeah, well, one day we were blood brothers," Rise said. "Now you sounding like brothers ain't brothers and blood ain't blood. What do I need to understand about that?"

"Yo, Rise, you know, sometimes we're not exactly seeing something but we know it's there," I said, forcing the words out, turning my eyes away from my friend. "But sooner or later you got to air it out before it gets really stink. You know what I mean?"

Lexi

"I hear you got some words in your mouth you need to get out," Rise said.

"Yeah. Right. So look, man. We've sat together—sometimes right here in this room—and talked about how foul drugs are. I remember you saying how they were bringing

Slovo

71

down life on the street and how you couldn't show any props for dudes on the nod. Now you running a whole new game. What's up with that?"

"What you see changes," Rise said. "I was seeing something different then than I do now. Just like all them dudes banging their veins in some hallway looking for a place to stick their needles. They weren't born on the nod, so they must have woke up one morning seeing something different than they seen before."

"What do you see different?" I asked.

"Me," Rise answered, his head down. "One day I seen me standing in the cold by the side of the track waiting for my train to come. All I was getting was colder and colder and my train never did come. What I'm thinking now is that I need to get out of the cold."

"Not just getting paid?"

"The paper go with the heat," Rise said. "I don't expect you to see it. You still waiting for that train to come. Deep in your heart you believe it's on its way. Going to take you right on out of here to the good life, right? We used to talk about that good life. What we were going to do, how we were going to tip and style like we owned the world. You remember that?"

"Yeah."

My train is coming.

"You still believe in it, or you looking the other way?"

"I don't know," I answered. "But I know you used to say that drugs were heaping pain on people. That's what you about? Heaping pain on people?"

"Drugs is a pain you can handle, little brother," Rise said. "That's why people out there looking for them. That's why they keep going back to them. It ain't fly, but it's real."

"I don't know, Rise. I don't know if everything you can touch is real."

"We're family, man. You and me." Rise tapped his chest and tapped mine. "When nobody digs your program, you turn to your family, to your brother. Ain't that right?"

"We're still brothers," I said. "I just have to wrap my mind around what's going on."

"I'm checking out your heart, Jesse," Rise said. "This is about real life, not about no dreams and stories. Real life, man. You can close your eyes and think about what you want to happen and what you want to see. But when you open your eyes, it's still the same old streets and the same old hurts. That's real life, and sooner or later you got to deal with it or walk away from it. I'm looking at you but I'm seeing me and feeling all warm, man. It's about the peace."

"It's about the peace," I said.

I packed my stuff up and said good-bye to Rise's

grandmother. When she smiled at me, I smiled back and felt a little foolish, because I didn't know what her smile meant or why I was smiling. Rise walked me downstairs and kept saying that he was real glad I was doing his biography.

"What did you think about Mason the other day?" I asked.

"Mason's gone," Rise said. "He's like a dead man who don't know he's dead, and still trying to walk around with the people and wondering why nobody's talking to him. He's catching an attitude because he thinks people are ignoring him, when all that's really wrong is that he's gone. He's a dead man sniffing around used-to-be. It's cold, but there it is."

What I was thinking as I was heading home was maybe Rise wasn't talking about Mason at all. Maybe he was talking about himself. Nothing that he had said before—about drugs killing the neighborhood and messing up people's lives—was out of his head. It all had to be there somewhere.

But I didn't want to walk away from him. I didn't want to put a name on it, to run it down to his face or walk around telling myself it was cool to turn my back on somebody I had cared for as much as I had for Rise. I told myself that if I did his autobiography right, if I did a really good job, maybe I could change him back to what I knew. Because the dude I knew would not have been dealing blow. I thought about him saying that dealing might lead to his portrait in chalk and me slipping under the police tape to put the chalk marker around his body. The thought was sadder than I wanted to carry, or even know about.

I was tight with my folks in a way. I could say things to them, and they would try not to get too crazy about it even if they were nervous. But there were things they didn't know about. It wasn't as if they were stupid or anything—it was like their brains were in a different place than mine sometimes. When I was young and had a cold, all I wanted was for Mom to take care of me—make me some soft-boiled eggs and feel my forehead with the palm of her hand. That was all good, and I enjoyed it without thinking too much about it. Mom enjoyed it too. But now that I'm older, I don't want her fussing over me, even when I'm sick, and she doesn't see it because her head is in a different place, or maybe in the same place but at the wrong time.

That's how I felt about Rise. If Rise wasn't doing well in school, I would have spoke to it, said something to Mom, and we would have talked about it. But how are you going to tell your parents something like "Hey, I think my blood brother is going to get into some big-time crime but I don't want you to say anything about it because it's all heavier than we can deal with"?

It was more complex, too. I had heard the whole rap about how we didn't grow drugs around the way. We didn't have no airplanes, so *somebody* had to bring them in and get them to the streets. All the needy veins ended at the fingertips—they didn't stretch to South America, or Afghanistan, or anyplace else they were growing the stuff. The people bringing in drugs weren't the kind of people you stood on the corner and pointed your finger at, either. They were the kind of people who shot you because it was easier than moving down the block.

I drew a five-panel cartoon. In the first panel my character Spodi Roti, the Rasta Blasta, came in from

school and told his mom that a crackhead jumped off the roof and his mom said, "That's so cute." In the next panel Spodi said he just found out the mailman was HIV positive and his mom asked him if his room was clean. In the third panel he asked her did she know if ammo from a .357 would fit a Kalishnakov, and his mom asked him if he could sing in it too. In the fourth panel Spodi says, "Sing in what?" and in the last panel his mom says, "Isn't that Greek you're speaking?"

Busted over to C.J.'s house for our Cuban band gig.

Benny was there, and he had two congas and a pile of shirts. The shirts were green with all this frilly stuff down the front that made them look more like blouses than men's shirts.

"Those are our outfits," C.J. said. "So we look like a real band."

"Yo, Benny, I told you I don't read music, right?"

"You don't have to worry about it," Benny said. "Just get on the conga and follow the piano. The more we play together, the better we're going to get. Check it out—I got my camera and I know this chick who's going to take pictures and everything. This is going to be smoking."

We put on the shirts and a waistband that came up too high on me and went over to the party. It was at this girl's house up on the hill, and it was cool except that her house was like something out of a magazine, it was so fine. Her father met us at the door and told us he wanted us to play for an hour and a half and then we could leave.

Benny asked him where the money was, and he told Benny we would get the money before we left. I wasn't worried that the guy didn't have the money because the house was so special, and I was thinking more about playing the conga because I didn't really know anything about that.

There were a bunch of okey-dokes at this girl's birthday party. All together there were about twenty-five kids and not one that I knew. I mentioned it to Benny as we set up.

"They're too classy for you, bro," he whispered.

They were, too. Only a few were black even though the people giving the party were dark-skinned. The rest were either white or Asian. I'm down with everybody, so that didn't bother me, but I always thought that Cubans were mostly black.

Benny introduced us as the Caballeros, which was cool, and this one guy started playing his conga but real low and real sweet, like he knew what he was doing. They were still giving us the fish eye as the rest of us started on the congas and the horns came in and didn't sound too tough because nobody knew what we were supposed to be playing. Then C.J. came in on the piano and you could see them straighten up. C.J. was cooking from the get-go, and they were just standing there looking at us. Then the birthday girl's father took her hand and started dancing, and the rest of them, the eight or nine who could dance a little, joined them.

Okay, so we played for almost two hours. C.J. was sounding so good that he made me believe I could play.

"Man, did you hear how that baby grand was sound-ing?" C.J. was saying on the way down the hill when the gig was over. "I need a new instrument."

"How about the church's piano?"

"It's so dull-sounding you want to bang it harder to try to get some life out of it," C.J. said. "I asked my moms about getting an electronic keyboard. Some of them are super bad. She don't believe in credit and so that's out, and she won't let me play in the band to make any money."

"You played today!"

"Right, because she found out who I was playing for—that dude works downtown in one of those big Wall Street companies. He was in *Ebony* and stuff."

"So what are you going to do?"

"She's got her heart on me going to college, but that's two years away. I think she hopes that I give up the music. Switch to something like accounting or business," C.J. said. "You know what she would really dig?"

"A preacher."

"You got it," C.J. said. "Then she could go on and die and figure she did her job with me."

"We're going to be the same way," I said. "I mean, when we grow up and have kids and stuff, we're going to be just like our folks, trying to tell them the right thing to do even when we don't want to listen to what they want."

"I'm not having any kids," C.J. said.

"You don't know that," I said. "You'll probably be one of these guys who have fifteen or sixteen kids."

I was feeling good and kind of light, but C.J. wasn't in the mood for being light. He was thinking about something else, and I figured it was serious, so I didn't push too hard.

"C.J., you were together today," I said. "You were

great. Nobody could have pulled this thing off except you, man."

"As far as it went." C.J. put his arm around me. "And as far as it goes, man. But we may just have to bust out of this joint."

I didn't know what that meant.

White Clara, Benny, Gun, and me were sitting on the stoop. White Clara was braiding Benny's hair and going on about some guy named Brittle who had a gun.

"Calvin said he had the gun stuck down in his pants, and they were so low his fly was touching the tops of his sneakers," she said. "And he ain't but like five or six or some ridiculous age."

"It was probably a cap gun," Benny said. "Lot of kids got cap guns that look real. Guy pulled a stickup in a bank downtown with a cap gun. They arrested him and he still had the box it came in and the receipt because he was going to take it back after the stickup."

"Calvin said it wasn't no cap gun," White Clara said.

I watched White Clara's fingers flying through Benny's hair. She wasn't really white, but so light-skinned she might as well have been.

"If a white cop sees you with a cap gun, he's going to use it as an excuse to shoot you," White Clara said.

"If I was a cop and I saw you with a gun that looked real, I'd shoot your butt, too," Benny said.

"What this school bus coming down this street for?" White Clara asked, pointing toward the corner. "They got school buses for summer school?"

I turned

Cap gun

and saw the bus start down the street, then speed up.

When the guys appeared at the window, all I could think was that they were some kind of ball team. Then I saw the do-rags and the glint of metal as they lifted their pieces over the bottoms of the school bus windows.

"Drive-by!" White Clara screamed, and went over the side rail as the first bullets hit the steps.

I panicked big-time and just closed my eyes and covered my head. Then I heard the bus squeal to a stop, and I thought the guys from inside were getting out and coming back after us. I opened my eyes and saw that the bus had stopped because a gypsy cab had pulled out in front of it.

The cabdriver was yelling at the bus driver; then he must have seen the guns, because he ran back to his cab as the shots rang out.

Pow! Pow! Pow! Pow! Pow! That fast. Then the driver of the bus hit the front of the gypsy cab and pushed it out of the way and sped down the street.

We looked around for White Clara and found her in the basement rubbing her hip.

"Man, I'm shot!" Benny was holding his hand.

I looked at it and saw that he had a hole in the palm of his hand between his forefinger and his thumb. I felt sick to my stomach.

I sat down and took deep breaths so I wouldn't throw

up. The pain was
getting to Benny,
and White Clara
was trying to keep
him calm. In the street a
crowd was beginning to
gather around the
gypsy cab. I didn't
want to look at
Benny's hand any-
more, so when I saw
Gun start over to the
cab, I went with him.
The driver was sitting outside the cab on the ground.

He was a big man, with a heavy belly that was heaving as he breathed. His face looked distressed and his
eyes were searching the crowd that gathered in front of
him. He was in a bad way and he knew it.

The whole thing depressed me. I went upstairs and
lay across the bed and wanted to cry, but crying felt so
stupid. This was real life, as Rise had said. And what the
heck did that mean?

The talk was that it was the Diablos, a gang from
uptown, that had done the shooting. What I knew about
them was that they took beatdowns to get into the gang
and worse beatdowns if they tried to get out. The saying
was that once you were a Diablo, you were in for life. It

91

was the first shooting of the week.

The second drive-by came two days later, and we heard about it in the usual way, a stream of police cars and emergency vehicles, sirens wailing, speeding through the hood, and turning up Frederick Douglass Boulevard. The first word was some wack garbage about terrorists, but then the cell phones started working and we got the news.

Some Diablos had been shot up really bad, and at least one of them had been seriously injured and could die. Everybody was out on the street and guessing if this was a payback shooting. Calvin said that he thought it was the Haitians, because the gypsy driver had been Haitian. I didn't think so, because they weren't into gangs, just making a living.

When Sidney came by and sat on the stoop with us, even the guys who talked about not wanting to hang with cops wanted to see what he had to say.

"These were professionals," Sidney said. "Nothing to do with gangs."

"What did it have to do with?" C.J. asked.

"We suspect drugs," Sidney said, shaking his head. "What else? Half of what goes on around here is about drugs, isn't it?"

Sidney split, and I told C.J. what Rise had said about dealing.

"You still hanging with him?" C.J. asked. "Because a lot of this mess is getting heavy. You start talking about Mason being in jail and Rise dealing—that's heavy."

"He's thinking about dealing," I said. "He's not dealing yet."

"You need to know what's going down," C.J. said.

"Why do I have to know right now?"

"Because . . . man." C.J. shrugged. "I don't know, I'm just so sick of all these drive-by shootings, the drugs, and all these games we're playing. You know what I mean?"

"Yeah, I guess I do," I said.

It turned out that I didn't have to call Rise. He called me. He asked me if I wanted to meet some "swinging" people.

"Like who?" I asked.

"Like some Spanish chicks I know," he said. "You down with meeting some new people? Maybe you can draw them or something."

"I don't know," I said.

"What? You scared?"

"No," I lied.

The place I was supposed to meet Rise was across from where the old Audubon Ballroom used to be. That's where Malcolm X was killed, and that was what I was thinking when I got off the bus.

11

"You the book-writing man?"

I nodded. The accent could have been Jamaican—I wasn't sure. What I was sure of was I didn't want to be in the Ras Uhuru Social Haven. The dim room was painted a hospital green. On the walls were pictures of Bob Marley and Haile Selassie. But it was the scent that overwhelmed me. It was a sickening competition between the burning incense sticks placed along the walls and the aerosol sprays that were supposed to remind you of some spring scene.

Two guys sat at a table near the door playing dominoes. The table leg had a scabbard taped to it, and the machete it held was half out. I made a mental note not to say anything bad about that table.

The guy who had met me at the door was very black, and blade thin. When he smiled—no, he didn't smile—when he showed his teeth, he reminded me of a program I had seen on *Animal Kingdom* when a lion had caught some animal and was looking him over before settling down to dinner. His eyes were no more than narrow slits, and what should have been the white parts looked more yellow than white.

He took me to a back room, where I found Rise having his nails done by a pretty brown-skinned woman. She looked to be about my mother's age.

"You bring the book?" Rise asked.

I said yes and nodded at the lady doing his nails as I laid my portfolio case on the table. The woman watched me and, when she saw some of the pictures I had inked, turned her head so she could see them better.

"What's that?" Rise turned the portfolio around to see a picture I had drawn of us playing the Junior Gauchos. Rise had been the star of the team up to then, and Gun had just been another player. But that game the Junior Gauchos were supposed to beat us easily, and they were doing it until the last few minutes, when Gun went crazy. He was throwing up shots from the outside and they were all falling. Rise was our big rebounder, and he kept getting the ball and passing to Gun and we came within one point of upsetting the Gauchos.

"I remember that game," Rise said. "That's when I realized my destiny. All I had to do was to step up and get it. If I had stepped up a few minutes earlier, we would have whipped the Gauchos. I learned something from that day."

"You did these pictures?" the woman asked, looking at me.

"Yeah, he did them," Rise said. "My man here is writing my autobiography. I'm living the life and he writing it down like I tell him."

"You're a good little artist," the woman said.

She inspected Rise's nails and then started putting her files and polish and stuff in her bag. Rise took a bill out of his shirt pocket and gave it to her. She smiled, put the money in her bra, and left.

"So I guess the Devils or whatever they be calling themselves won't be coming around our hood anymore," Rise said, inspecting his nails. The way he did it, putting his fingers out and spreading them under the light, was supposed to impress me. I knew that.

"I heard one of them was killed," I said.

"When you play the big game, you pay the big price," Rise said. "But I didn't have a choice. I can't let people think they can show disrespect in my hood. You know what I mean?"

"You did the drive-by?"

"I dropped the word," Rise said. "Let's go over some more of your pictures. You see how the girl who was doing my nails was checking out the drawings? That's the thing you got to be about. You got to get the ink on the

WORD

paper or else you ain't been here. You know what I mean?"

I didn't believe Rise. You could hear his style on any rap jam and even get down with the gangsta lean he was fronting. It made me a little mad, but I was still nervous about being in the place as he started looking at my drawings.

"What's this picture?"

"That's the time you and me and Calvin went down to Atlantic City with Calvin's parents—"

"Snap! And Calvin stood on the boardwalk and said he could see Africa and we believed him!" When Rise laughed, he looked young again. I hadn't noticed that he didn't look young anymore.

"I went to school and told the teacher I had been to Africa over the weekend. You know me, I had to build it up a little. I didn't just see Africa—I ran down I had *been* to Africa."

"Yeah, I remember that too," I said. "Look, Rise, you talking about drive-bys and people getting—you know—don't that freak you out, man?"

Rise leaned back in his chair. "Truthfully?" he asked. "Yeah, it do. I don't, like, stay up nights and whatnot, but like I know that if I can ride the pony long enough, I can make it to where I want to be. You know what I mean?"

"Who are those guys outside?"

"You don't want to know them," Rise said. "You

don't want to talk to them too tough. They're all mechanics. If something is wrong, they know how to fix it, make it right. That's all you need to know. They giving me the downtown area. From 147th to 141st. That's all mine now."

My mind was going blank. The whole thing was too heavy for me. I couldn't even think straight, but Rise wanted to keep going over the pictures as if him "dropping the word" for a drive-by wasn't any big thing. If it wasn't big to him, it was sure big to me. Most of the drawings were just sketches, and he was telling me that I should finish them. I told him we had to decide which ones we wanted to use.

"I'll get with you later on that," he said. "You just keep doing the pictures. Yeah, and don't be repeating anything I said to you. You got that?"

"I got it."

A knock came on the door and a heavyset man stuck his head in and told Rise that Tania wanted to see him. Rise told him to send her in.

"I want you to meet this girl," he said to me. "She's sweet, but I can't deal with her. You got an old lady?"

"Not really," I said.

"You can have Tania," Rise said.

Tania came in. She was about my age but dressed like maybe she was older so I couldn't tell. And she was as fine as she wanted to be and knew it. Rise introduced us, and she looked me up and down like she was thinking of buying me or something. Rise got up, closed my portfolio, and asked me to bring him some finished pictures.

"Color and everything," he said. "When can you have them done? Next week?"

"Yeah."

"Okay," he said. "I'll see you next week. Tania's going with you. Y'all be nice to each other. I got some work to do."

Tania started to protest, and Rise held his hand up in front of her face and she stopped in the middle of her sentence.

Me and Tania left—went through the murky part of the club and out into the cool evening air.

"So where we going?" she asked.

"I don't know," I said.

"You ain't nothing but a kid, right?" she asked, smiling.

"How old are you?" I asked.

"Fourteen," she said, running her hands down the front of her jeans, "but I got it going on, baby. Didn't you notice?"

"Yeah, I guess so."

"You guess so? You got to say it. Say, 'Tania, you got it going on!'"

"You got it going on!"

"Look at you, all embarrassed and everything," she said. "You want to go get something to eat?"

I said yes.

Tania was crazy cute. She had almond-shaped eyes and looked at you from the corners of them as if she knew more than she was saying. Her face was pretty when she was talking, but when she smiled, it just warmed up the distance between us. I was answering her smile with a stupid grin of my own and I knew she was about twenty hundred years older than me in some ways. She didn't just have it going on, she had it just about finished.

She had some money, a lot in fact, and we went to a Chinese restaurant between 155th and 154th. We sat in a booth, and the waitress, who knew Tania, came over and asked her if she wanted her shrimps and fries. Tania said yes. I ordered vegetable fried rice.

"So what do you do?" she asked.

"Mostly draw," I said.

"Those your pictures?"

I was glad to open the portfolio and show her the pictures. She called over the waitress.

"Jesse, this is Connie. Connie, this is Jesse. Connie has a regular name and a Chinese name. Her Chinese name is Kang-Ni, which I think is cool, but she don't like it because it's Chinese."

"Who did the pictures?" Connie asked.

"Jesse did. He's doing a story about Rise or something."

"His autobiography," I said.

Connie looked the pictures over and then told me to put them up so I wouldn't get anything on them. She said I should sell them.

The food came, and Tania told me that if I was ever uptight for something to eat, I could come here and Connie would fix me up.

"We used to go to school together," Tania said. "I don't go to school anymore."

"How come?"

"'Cause it's not happening," Tania said. "You know, you go to school and they try to teach you stuff, and then you come out and you find that all you going to be doing is what your daddy did if you're a boy and what your mama did if you're a girl. My mama ain't never did diddly, and I'm going down that same road, so I might as well keep it real. You know what I mean?"

"You just can't wake up one morning and make a decision about your whole life," I said. "You don't know what's going to happen."

"Yeah, I do. You look around and tell me what you see." Tania had a grain of rice on her chin. "Connie was always talking about how she was going to be a doctor. Now she says she's probably going to be working right here next to her mama. That's the way it goes, man."

"That's a hard way to look at things," I said.

"I'm not saying that school is just all the way wack,

but you got to figure out what you got to work with. It's got its place and everything. But if all you're going to do is hang in the hood, it don't mean nothing. All they doing on my block is halfway surviving, sometimes thriving, but mostly jiving. You ain't but a kid, but I know you can get next to that."

"So what you doing? You jiving or thriving?" I asked.

"I'm just doing that one-day-at-a-time shuffle." Tania suddenly teared up and we got quiet. She had been looking right at me, but now she looked away. I didn't feel like eating anymore.

There was a calendar on the wall with a pretty Chinese girl on it. Her hair was jet black and seemed to catch some of the red from her dress. The numbers on the calendar were printed in red and black, but it was a completely different red from the girl's dress. The dress was a deep red, and you could see other colors in it too. The numbers were flat, just there.

"So you want to make a picture of me?" Tania asked. "Sure."

"We'll go to my house." Tania put a ten-dollar bill on the table. "Right down the street."

Tania's house was real bad. There was a guy sitting in the downstairs hall with a baseball bat leaning against the wall next to him. Tania called him Billy and said that he was there to keep the crackheads out. There was an elevator, but we walked up three flights to her apartment.

She unhooked her keys from her belt and unlocked the door. Her place was neat and smelled a lot better than the hallway. From the hallway we had come into the kitchen. Over the stove there was a row of yellow porcelain jars with green trim. The first read FLOUR, then SUGAR, COFFEE, and TEA.

Tania took my hand and led me into her room. There were pictures of Marilyn Monroe on the walls and a poster of her standing on the sidewalk with her dress blowing up.

"You want me to take my clothes off so you can draw me?" Tania asked.

"No," I said.

"You going to hit on me?"

"I thought I was just going to draw you," I said, feeling mucho stupid.

"That's okay." Tania looked in the mirror. "But if Rise asks me, I'm going to say we did it, okay?"

"Yeah."

My face was flushing and I was trying hard to keep cool. I kept telling myself that all I wanted to do was to draw Tania, but all kinds of images rushed through my head. I did want to draw Tania, but the way she talked, as if I could have done anything else, was messing with my mind.

When I draw a picture, I'm not that interested in making it look exactly like what I'm drawing. My dad likes that—to see a picture and say something about how it looks almost like a photograph. But what I want is to draw a picture where I can see more about what I drew than just what it looks like. But with Tania I wanted the picture to look just like her so she would like it. I wanted her to like me, too.

Tania sat on the bed, and I sat on one chair and used a straight-back chair for an easel. As I started to draw her, the first few lines, the curve of her eyebrows away from the bridge of her nose, were almost perfect. I knew I could do a good picture if I didn't mess it up by getting into my "artist" thing. Sometimes I wanted people to see me being an artist and acting like an artist, and I would mess pictures up. But with Tania's picture, the two of us in the room alone with no one to see us, I concentrated on the marks I was making on the paper. I was feeling it and it was feeling good.

It seemed like a short time, but when I had finished, Tania said I had been drawing over a half hour.

"So what do you think?" I asked.

She looked at it for a while and then turned it so that it was next to her face as she looked into the mirror. "Can I have it?" she asked in a voice that sounded like a little kid's. "Please."

"Sure, I did it for you."

She looked at me and then she kissed me, putting both of her arms around my neck.

TANIA

"You want me to do anything?" she said, making a gesture toward the bed.

"No," I said, mad at myself because I was scared.

"I don't think I can get boys like you to like me," Tania said. "You want to be all good and everything, right?"

"I like you."

"You don't have to feel bad about that," she said. "I don't want to be like no Miss Skippy Skank, either. You going to go home and think about me sometime?"

"Yeah."

"It's okay if I tell Rise we did it?"

"Yeah."

She walked me to the door. There was an old woman sitting in the kitchen. Her face was a thousand wrinkles and old, but her eyes were hard. Tania spoke to her in Spanish. I couldn't understand what she was saying, but the tone seemed sharp.

She pushed me out the door with one hand and leaned against the wall. "You want to kiss me again?" she asked.

I kissed her—or maybe she was doing most of the kissing, because her mouth was really busy. "I got a lot of business I take care of," she said softly. "But if you don't mind that, I could be your old lady. What you think?"

"Fine," I said, not really knowing what she meant about a lot of business.

She smiled and stood in the doorway as I started down the stairs.

Kissing Tania had been hot, and I couldn't think about anything except how it felt to have her tongue in my mouth and her body against mine. My heart was still jumping as I got outside and saw that it was already dark.

When I got upstairs, Mom asked me where I had been and I told her that I had been to see Rise and then stopped at a girl's house.

"What girl?"

"I just met her," I answered. "I drew a picture of her at her house."

"She had her clothes on?" Mom leaned her head over to one side and gave me a look.

"Yeah. Is that all girls think about?" I asked. "Taking their clothes off if you draw them?"

"I was just wondering," she said, turning away. "Go wash up for supper."

I had had the Chinese food but I still had some room for supper. As I washed up, I thought about Rise and what he had said. He looked the same, but the way he was acting, even the way his voice sounded, it wasn't the same Rise I had in my head. I wasn't sure whether he was only acting different or if he was different, but I didn't know how a person could be different. Not so suddenly, anyway.

RiSE?

The word on the street is that Rise is taking over the whole neighborhood." I could tell C.J. was breathing hard, even over the telephone. "They say that the drug dealers from up in the Heights gave him the territory, and they were the ones that shot that dude on 145th and Convent."

"What did you do? Run up the stairs to get to the phone?" I asked.

"No, man, I just wanted to let you know what Calvin said," C.J. said. "I think I've seen at least two of those dudes from the Heights on television. They're violent as anything. Calvin said they'd shoot you and make bets on how you going to fall."

"Rise told me that, but it doesn't have anything to do with us," I said, checking myself out in my dresser mirror.

"It does if Rise is still a Count," C.J. said. "But I'm telling you this. If the police start rounding up all the Counts, I'm going to rat you out for a lighter sentence."

"Thanks, buddy, but I haven't done anything yet," I said.

"Police don't know that, so I'm still ratting you out," C.J. said.

"Yo, C.J., I thought you and me were tight."

"Yeah, but I need to get a light sentence, and you're the only Count I have a chance of beating."

"C.J., you couldn't beat me if I was an egg and you were a Mixmaster or something," I said. "You might have a chance against Little Man, but there's no way you're going to stand up against Jesse the Magnificent."

"Oh, I forgot to tell you something. Check this out." C.J. lowered his voice. "You remember when somebody was saying that there was this kid around with a gun? They said his name was Brittle or something like that? Well, the story now is that it was Little Man. He's carrying."

"You got a job with the *Amsterdam News*?" I asked. "How come you know everything?"

"People come to me with news," C.J. said. "They count on me for leadership."

"C.J., you still have some of your baby teeth," I said. "You're no leader. Take it from an older man, okay?"

"Well, check this out," C.J. said.

GOT THE NEWS

"I'm bringing the news to you—you're not bringing it to me."

"Hey, C.J., how did Calvin get all this information?"

"He told me that he saw Rise in the drugstore on Seventh Avenue and he told him."

"That's funny, because he told me the same thing and told me not to be spreading it around."

"So what's going on?"

"I don't know, C.J., I don't know."

Mom was calling, so I told C.J. I had to split for dinner.

At dinner Dad still had his foot propped up from when he had hurt it. Mom had made crab cakes, his favorite dish, and was being all nice to him as if he had done something wonderful by hurting his foot.

"Whatever you're thinking about, it must be amusing," Mom said as she laid the portobello mushrooms on my plate. "Sitting there smiling to yourself like a Chessy cat."

"You know what I was thinking?" Dad interrupted with his usual prelecture question. "I was thinking that if you were lying dead someplace, and a hungry chicken or a hungry pig came up on you, they would eat you faster than you could say lickety split."

I knew where he was going. "Well, that's them, and I'm me," I said.

"Archie, do we need that tonight?" Mom asked.

HUNGRY!

"I'm not saying anything about the boy," Dad answered. "I was just noticing a simple fact. Jesse doesn't eat meat, but some of the meat he don't eat would eat him! Now, is it wrong for me to notice a simple fact in life? Is that wrong?"

"No, dear, it's not wrong." Mom had answered in her you-*know*-that's-wrong voice, and Dad shut up.

It didn't bother me that Dad made fun of me not eating meat. He didn't really make that big a deal of it, so it wasn't a bother. But he was pouting and the dinner grew quiet.

I thought of Rise some more. He told me he didn't want me to repeat what he had said, but then he went ahead and told Calvin the same thing he had told me. When Calvin ran it back at me, it sounded more like everyday news, and that was a big thing. I was living in a hood with a lot of drugs and shootings, but I didn't want it to be every-day news. I figured me and my peeps all had something else going on that kept us out of that "everyday news" category. Now Rise looked like he was anxious to get into it.

I hated drugs. Almost everything that was going down wrong in the hood was based on people dealing. In school we were reading Dante's *Inferno*, which I did not like at all

Dante

except for the parts about going down to hell and seeing the different kinds of people there. What I thought was that sometimes, in the morning when the druggies were just reaching the streets and looking for the money to get their first hit of the day, it had to be like some kind of hell.

When crack was boss, the heads were jumpy and sometimes glassy-eyed as they tried to hunt down their rocks. That was a bad scene. But now that Boy was boss, and the hardest heads were mainlining the heroin, it was worse. They looked so foul—bent-over guys nodding out on the corner, women leaning against a building like they were half asleep, and dudes on crutches who were druggies and messed up with AIDS. Sometimes the corner of 149th Street looked like an ad for some desperate Third World country. All you had to do was put a sign over the street saying "Give to UNICEF" or something. And walking among them all, like vultures waiting for the dying to fall, were the dealers hustling the misery.

It scared me. The same way that seeing a dead kid lying in a coffin scared me. Seeing dead kids scared me because it made me know I could die. And seeing Rise on the deal made me feel the same way.

I tried to get my mind

off of it and asked Mom if she needed help with the dishes. She asked me why I assumed she was going to be doing the dishes at all.

"I know Bigfoot's not going to do them," I said.

"What you say?" Dad raised his voice.

"I'm sorry, Dad, it just came out funny," I said.

"Your mama's not going to say anything about you showing me disrespect," he said. "But just let me state something to you that's an absolute fact, and she's on my case before the words get out."

Dad humphed him a few humphs! and turned sideways in his chair to let the world know he had been mistreated.

Mom signaled me to leave and I sneaked off quietly. As I left she was giving him the poor-baby treatment. I knew he would pretend to ignore her even though he liked it.

I was feeling really down and got out my drawing pad to cheer myself up. What I thought I would do with Rise's autobiography was to put me in it as me and also as my favorite character, Spodi Roti.

In the first panel, I had a picture of a man slipping on a banana peel. In the second panel I had a woman tripping over her dog's leash. In the third panel I had a kid falling off a skateboard. Next, Spodi Roti and Wise are walking, and Spodi is saying "People are too careless, mon. They don't look where they going and always

SPODI
*ROTI
&WISE

PEOPLE ARE TOO CARELESS, MON. THEY DON'T LOOK WHERE THEY GOING AND ALWAYS FALLING AND KILLING THEMSELVES.

NAW, MON, THEY'RE OKAY. 'CAUSE SEEIN' AIN'T THE ONLY THING TO DO AND STANDIN' UP AIN'T THE ONLY THING THAT'S TRUE.

falling and killing themselves."

Wise says, "Naw, mon, they're okay. 'Cause seein' ain't the only thing to do and standin' up ain't the only thing that's true."

The thing was that me and Rise were blood brothers, but sometimes I really didn't know him. I remembered a time when he and I were sitting on the stoop when Drew came and sat down with us.

"What's going on?" Rise said.

"Nothing going on," Drew said. "I been sitting on this stoop for twenty years waiting for something to be going on. Things go by. Sometimes things don't make it by, but ain't nothing going on for Drew."

"Man, why don't you shut up with that garbage," Rise said.

At the time Drew was at least thirty and Rise wasn't more than fifteen. There was no way he could have beaten Drew, so I didn't know why he was running his mouth like that. Neither did Drew.

"Don't let your lip carry you no place

GARBAGE!

your hip can't get you out of, boy." That's what Drew said.

When Rise jumped up and squared off like he was ready to throw down, I was surprised, and so was Drew. Drew stood up real slow, reached behind him, and pulled out a straight razor. He flipped it open and just laid it alongside his leg. Rise looked at that razor, spit on the ground, and started off down the street. I got up and followed him.

I caught Rise on the corner of Malcolm X Boulevard and 147th Street. I asked him what was the matter.

"I hate dudes like that," he said. "Waste all their lives sitting on the stoop and still got to run their mouths."

I didn't know what he was talking about. Drew wasn't a superhero or anything, but he was like most of the people on the block, no special place to go and no special time to get there. It wasn't what I wanted for my life, and I understood that Rise wasn't wanting to go that way, either. I could get next to all that, but what I didn't get next to was why Rise was so upset that he had to step to a hard dude like Drew.

When I thought back to that, I wondered if maybe I didn't know Rise the way I thought I did.

I lay across the bed and did some more sketches of Spodi Roti even though I had promised myself fifty leben times I would stop drawing while I was lying on my back.

13

Another Teen—Another Funeral

That's what the headline read. The paper was reporting the funeral of the Diablo who had been wounded. He had died, and they were having his funeral at a storefront church in the Bronx where his grandmother lived. There was the usual picture, kind of fuzzy, of the kid standing with some friends in front of his house.

"He was a good boy." His grandmother was quoted in the paper right under his picture. "He is looking down from heaven now."

Farther down in the article it said the mayor was going to get tough on street crime.

On the stoop Gun said we all had to be careful because the Diablos might try to get revenge. "Especially since the story made the white papers," Gun was saying as he spun his basketball in his hands. I hadn't noticed before how long his fingers were, or how close to the color of the ball they were.

"My father said he sure wasn't looking down from heaven," White Clara said. "Because black people don't get to heaven."

"Your father is a wack head!" Gun said. "That's almost as bad as a crackhead except you don't have to pay for your high—it just comes natural with your empty head."

"Gun, did your mama have any children that lived?" White Clara asked.

"It don't matter if he's looking down from heaven or not," C.J. said. "No matter how you look at it, he's dead. Like the paper said—another teen, another funeral."

"His grandmother is just trying to make him look good," Gun said. "You can't blame her for that. I bet if he knew he was in the white papers, he'd be happy with it himself."

"How you going to be happy when you wake up and find yourself dead?" C.J. asked. "That's stupid, man."

"No, that's not stupid," White Clara said. "If you're dead and you're waking up, now that's stupid!"

Calvin came up and gave everybody except White Clara, who he didn't get along with, a high five. Gun asked him if he had seen the piece in the paper. Calvin said no and sat down and read it.

"I heard the Diablos are running scared, man," Calvin said. "Benny's cousin went to the funeral, and she said there were more reporters than people who came to see the dude off. You know those dudes who did him are bad. You're not messing with no wannabes and no junior varsity bangers. They're some stone-cold killers. They kill you and hand out their business cards at your funeral."

"This stuff is making me nervous," I said. "It's like things are going down—"

"—and we're like all up in it." Calvin finished my sentence. "I'm just thinking maybe we ought to stay off the block for a while. When they do their drive-bys, they know where to come looking."

"Everybody's getting nervous." Gun stretched his legs out in front of him. "My folks were talking it up big-time last night."

MOUTH

"What you thinking about Rise?" I asked. "You thinking he's getting in too deep?"

"You got to watch who you talking in front of," Calvin said. "Clara ain't nothing but mouth."

"I'm going on home." Clara stood up and pulled the bottom of her top down over her stomach. "All you guys are wannabes if you ask me."

"I didn't hear nobody asking you," Calvin said.

Clara had this little thing she does, turning her back and flipping up her dress at people. She did it and walked on down the block.

Calvin didn't say anything for a while, and I was wondering if I should ask him again about Rise, but I wasn't sure.

"Yo, here comes the Man!" C.J. said as a car pulled up real fast in front of the house.

Calvin jumped up and started running down the street, and I spun around and half crawled and half leaped into the vestibule. I banged my knee and stumbled as something brushed past me. I got to the stairs and felt my arm being grabbed. I tried to twist around and get my leg up when I felt the barrel of the gun against my cheek.

"Don't move, punk!" The white dude with his knee in my chest and his gun in my face pulled his badge from inside his shirt. "What's going on?"

"I thought you were a drive-by or something," I said.

"What you pulling up like that for?"

He told me to shut up and started patting me down. He didn't find any weapons, so he let me stand up. Another cop found Gun hiding under the stairs and pulled him out. C.J. and Calvin were outside in handcuffs when we got out to the stoop.

"I told you it was the cops," C.J. said. "What you run for?"

"You didn't say cops—you said the Man," Calvin said. "How I know what man your butt was talking about?"

After the cops figured out why we were running, they started laughing like it was some big joke. I didn't think it was funny. They asked us if we dug drive-bys, and we said no. At least me and C.J. and Gun said no; Calvin was mad and didn't say anything.

"You guys know anything about the guy who was killed?" the cop who had put his gun in my face asked.

We told him we didn't know anything, and he acted as if he didn't believe us. He asked us if we would call him if we got any information, and C.J. said we would call Sidney.

"Keeping it among the brothers, huh?"

"Whatever," Calvin said.

They ran down a thing about how one of these days it's going to be a real drive-by and one of us would be lying in a pool of blood crying for his mama.

We didn't answer him.

"You know what I do when some brother gets shot and is lying on the ground waiting for an ambulance that is probably going to get to the scene too late?" he asked. "Usually I have coffee. I know all the coffee spots around here. All I have to do is to walk into a place and say that I have a bleeder, and they know I have to wait at least five or ten minutes before I get back in the car, so I get my coffee free. That's one of the perks of the job. Cool, huh?"

The cops handed each one of us a card, and we made a big thing about throwing them away. It was a big thing because I was sitting on the stoop, copping an attitude that was chill to the world while inside I was, like, shaking. My heart was pumping hard and my knees felt like rubber. And while all this was going on, me trying to look

126

like I was ready to throw my hands in the air like I just didn't care while things were falling apart inside, I was checking myself out. It was like I was there, living in the moment, but I was also there digging myself and how I was pretending not to be terrified.

The truth was when the cop grabbed me in the hall-

way, I thought he was a Diablo and my life was over. For a few seconds the fear I had felt had just filled me up, had flared up into every part of me. My hands were stiff with fear, my heart was racing, my gut was turning, I was sweating.

DOWN the DRAIN

When I went upstairs, nobody was home. I locked the door, went to my room, and lay across the bed. I was exhausted. And the thing was that it didn't make any difference that it wasn't me who shot the dead Diablo. The thing was that the dead dude and me were caught up in the same sink with the stopper out, and the two of us swirling around toward the drain. He had gone down the dark hole, already disappearing from view, and I was going round and round, faster and faster, toward the same place.

14

I didn't remember falling asleep, and was surprised when I felt Mom shaking my shoulder and rubbing the tip of my nose with her finger to wake me.

"It's Sidney Rock calling," she said. "I think he's got baseball tickets." There was a smile in her voice.

It was nearly five thirty. I stumbled to the phone and listened as Sidney apologized about our run-in with the white cops.

"They're okay," he said. "Things are just too clearly defined for them sometimes. Not enough grays in their thinking."

"No big deal," I said.

"I was just wondering," Sidney said. "I don't know if I've told you this, but I can always get baseball tickets. Nosebleed seats, usually, but they're free. If you ever want them, just let me know."

"Yeah, okay."

"How's your piece about Rise coming?"

The question caught me off guard. I asked him how he knew I was doing Rise's life, and he said a guy uptown he knew told him about it.

"It's okay," I said.

He reminded me about the tickets again before he hung up.

I knew what he was doing. He was telling me that Rise was hanging with a dangerous crew and he knew about it. These weren't regular people, the kind who took the buses early in the morning to work, or who worked hard all day downtown; these were the kind who wore expensive clothing and flashy gold chains around their necks and looked at you with slitty eyes.

"So you going to the ball game with Sidney?" Mom asked.

"Now how can I go to the ball game with a cop?" I asked. "Suppose I'm sitting in the stands with this dude and find out he's overly programmed. Some ballplayer takes off from first and slides into second and the scoreboard starts flashing SB-SB-SB. He turns to me and asks me what that means and I say stolen base."

"And he runs out onto the field and arrests the player?" Mom finished it.

"Yeah."

"Jesse, have I ever told you that you get your intelligence from your father's side?"

"What he get from you?" Dad was washing up in the

kitchen sink, which Mom hated.

"Good looks and charm," Mom said. "Don't you think so?"

At the table they were joking around for a while about what genes I had inherited, and then they got into it again about who was doing what chores around the house. I didn't mind them arguing until the end, when Mom started crying and Dad was getting mad.

"You want me to do all the cleaning and cooking, I'll do it!" He raised his voice some more. "I'll quit my job and stay home and be the housewife, because I sure can't be no man around this house."

He got up and left the table, and a moment later I heard the bedroom door slam.

"He left his plate just where it was sitting," Mom said. "But at least with his sore foot he couldn't stomp off. I need to learn how to draw so I can show him just how stupid he looks. I should leave his plate right there for the rest of our lives together."

I got up and put Dad's plate in the sink. There was something going on between them, and I didn't know what it was. I knew it wasn't anything about washing dishes, but Dad was upset about something. Sooner or later it would come out, and I just hoped it was nothing serious. Dad couldn't express his ideas as easily as Mom could, and I think that pissed him off sometimes.

Mom was watching television and Dad was still sulking

in the bedroom when the idea came to me. I got out my pad and made some quick sketches, but nothing came the way I wanted it. I remembered seeing a poster of Huey Newton, the old Black Panther, sitting on a chair with a gun next to it and him looking like a king or something.

When I had first seen the picture of Huey Newton, it made me think of a king, but when I saw a documentary on the Black Panthers and saw him in his house with that same picture on the wall, I thought that what I was really seeing was him trying to look like some kind of hero. I started drawing, first from memory, then went to a book that had a photograph of the Huey Newton poster and used that as reference.

My picture of Rise sitting on a high-back wicker chair was good. I thought about calling him up and taking it over to him even though it was getting late. I decided not to.

Sometimes when I sleep on a picture, when it's in my mind all night, I see it differently than when I'm first working on it. That was the thing with the picture of Rise. In the morning it was still good, but it wasn't what I wanted. The proportions were right, and Rise was looking like a very satisfied image of himself, but that wasn't what I had intended.

I messed with the picture a little, putting lines here and there, adding some shading around the face, even adding some abstract figures. But it still wasn't right, and this time I knew what I really wanted.

When I began again, it wasn't with a lot of quick sketches or hurried marks on the open paper. It was slow, with the chair in the center of the paper and then Rise on it. He was huge, with his head bigger in proportion than it could ever be in life, and his teeth showing in a half smile as he snarled from the flatness of the page.

"*Why you do me like this?*" I imagined him saying. "*Why you making me look like some kind of freak?*"

I had a little hologram, about the size of a nickel, of a skull, and I painted a ring on his finger and pasted the death head onto it.

The paper was twenty inches by twenty-four and heavy, and I remembered an old frame that I had on top of the closet. I got the frame down, slid out the picture of Muhammad Ali, slipped in Rise, and put the picture on my dresser so I could take a good look at it.

It still wasn't right. There was too much white space around the edges. I took it out of the frame and filled in the white areas with silver paint. The silver wasn't exactly right, because it toned the picture down too much. I hadn't expected that. So then I put some highlights in Rise's eyes, yellow and red to suggest flames. That was boss. That was definitely on the money.

Mom knocked on the door as I was setting up the fan to dry the paint a little.

"What is that?" Mom asked.

"What do you think it is?" I asked.

"It looks a little bit like your father first thing in the morning," she said, her head to one side.

"Mom!"

"Don't tell him I said that—I don't feel like babying him all day," she said. "Well, it could be Bizarro, the mad villain of Gotham City, Stinky Scourge of the Underworld contemplating his stockpile of weapons of mass destruction."

"I like that," I said. "Stinky Scourge of the Underworld."

"Or some other monster," Mom said. "Don't leave it on the dresser tonight. You'll wake up and scare yourself to death."

Mom asked me if I wanted breakfast without guessing who was in the picture. I let it go and skipped the breakfast. I wanted Rise to see it as soon as possible.

15

Rise was in the shower when I got to his house. His mother and grandfather were at the kitchen playing pitty-pat for pennies. There were paper cups on the table and an ashtray in front of Mrs. Davis that was piled with discarded cigarettes. She was in her housecoat with her hair up in brown-paper rollers. The kitchen window was closed, and the air had the faint smell of burned hair grease.

"So what you doing with yourself these days, Jesse?" Rise's mother asked.

"Just hanging out, mostly," I said. "Trying to stretch the summer out."

"I can hear that," she said. "Marvin, you got any eights over there?"

"Play and find out." Rise's grandfather leaned back in his chair and smiled. "You can never tell what I'm holding, girl."

"What's Rise doing in the shower so long?" Mrs.

Davis asked. "He knows Jesse's out here waiting for him. He spends as much time cleaning himself as Mama does cleaning the house."

"I don't mind waiting," I said. I had put the picture in Rise's room on the dresser.

Mr. Johnson smiled, put his last three cards facedown on the table, then turned them up one by one. "Why people got to be in a hurry to get their beating?" he asked, pulling in the small pile of pennies in the middle of the table.

Mrs. Davis looked at her cards, sucked her teeth, and started dealing again. Mr. Johnson looked at his cards. "Woman, who taught you how to deal?"

Rise came out of the shower and got dressed. By that time I had changed my mind about the picture I had made. When I did it, when I drew the picture and colored it, I thought I was making an image of Rise that he would see and get puzzled over. He would wonder why I had made him look so strange, and I imagined myself explaining to him that, in my eyes, he was changing.

"You're becoming a different person," I imagined myself saying. *"Somebody I almost don't know. That's why I drew you that way. You're not the same person I grew up with and who was my blood brother."*

But waiting for Rise, sitting with his mom and his grandfather, I could feel myself growing more and more tense. Rise was going to be mad, I thought.

Then it came to me that maybe it wasn't so much how Rise had changed his appearance, after all. Maybe what was wrong was really about me and how I was seeing Rise. With everything going on, the shootings and the way Rise was acting, I was looking to make things right again, to get back to what I was comfortable with. That was the old Rise and the old hanging out. Looking at Rise, thinking about him, was like going to a horror movie and seeing an evil doll that killed people. It was familiar and unfamiliar at the same time. And it was the unfamiliar, the not knowing how a doll could talk or think, or how someone I had known for so long could deal drugs, that made it so depressing.

"Yo, Jesse!" Rise came out of his room wearing slacks and a T-shirt and holding up the picture. "This is me, man! Truth rules, little brother. Truth rules!"

He started showing the picture to his mom and his grandfather. All the time, he was telling them how great it was. His grandfather said something about me being the best artist he knew, and his mom was talking about how good the colors stood out. I knew they were coming from what Rise was saying, his enthusiasm. He was holding the picture with both hands, as if he didn't even want to let it get out of his possession.

I wanted to see it again myself.

16

T ania called.

"So you don't have a girlfriend, right?" she asked.

"I guess not," I said.

"You guess? You don't know if you got an old lady or not?"

"Okay, then I don't," I said.

"Okay, then you do," she said. "I'm going to be your girlfriend from now on. You don't have to buy me nothing, or even take me out. All you got to do is be nice to me and talk to me sometimes. All right?"

"Sure," I said. "But how come you decided you wanted to be my girlfriend?"

"Well, you're not too good-looking, but you're sweet and you don't know so much about me you're going to be tramping me out and stuff," Tania said. "So we can make it. Except I don't want you to start going out with other girls so I don't have to beat them up or anything. That's, like, respect."

"Okay."

"I love you."

"I love you, too," I said.

She said good-bye and hung up.

That was the first time I ever told a girl that I loved her. And even though I really didn't know Tania, I liked having her for my girlfriend. I liked having a girlfriend. Period. Maybe I even loved her.

I was getting dressed and trying to figure out who I was going to tell that I had a girlfriend when C.J. called. He asked me if I would come over to the church. He sounded upset, and I asked him what was wrong. He said nothing, but the way he said it I figured it had to be heavy.

What I thought it was about was that his moms had put down him playing with our little Cuban band.

As I was putting on my sneakers, my mind was jumping back and forth between Tania, and how she was kind of a needy person who could really use a friend, and thinking about sex. She had said that she had it going on, and she did. But she also said she didn't want to be tramped out, and I could dig that.

I thought C.J.'s mom—she was the main person in his family—should have let him play in the band. C.J. was good on the piano and on the organ. He couldn't do anything else that I knew about.

When I got to the church, Elder Smitty was there. His

real name was Arthur Smith, but all the kids called him Elder Smitty. Tall and broad shouldered, it was easy to imagine him swinging a big hammer or lifting a piano. He walked slowly, and always looked tired or as if he had pains in his legs when he moved them. But on Sunday mornings, when the sermon got good to him and seemed to lift his body up and make his step lighter, he looked twenty years younger. When he didn't shave, his white whiskers gleamed against his black face and he could have posed for a picture of the black king that came and saw Christ.

Elder Smitty had retired from driving a moving van and spent a lot of his time taking care of the church. When I walked in, he was sitting in the front pew, a broom standing between his legs.

C.J. was sitting on the piano bench and Little Man was sitting next to him. I nodded toward Elder Smitty and went up to where C.J. and Little Man were.

"He teaching me to play the piano." Little Man looked up at me.

"I didn't know you could play at all," I said.

"Check this out," Little Man said.

He started banging on the keys, not even trying to play anything, and grinning. I looked at C.J. and he looked miserable. I could see what was going on. Little Man was just messing with C.J.

After a minute he stopped and looked at C.J. and

asked him wasn't that good.

"No, it's not," I said. "You can't play for nothing."

"I didn't ask you," he said.

"I'm telling you," I said. "You can't play for nothing."

He stood up and got as close to me as he could, trying to punk me down.

"You want to step to me?" I asked him. "Let's go outside and get to stepping."

He started laughing again and moved back. "I don't have time for no lames," he said.

Little Man jumped off the platform, grabbed his jacket off the pew next to Elder Smitty, and strutted down the middle aisle to the front door. All the time, he had his hand up giving us the bird without turning around.

"Don't worry about it none," Elder Smitty said. "He's just trying to bring you down to his level. That's all he's trying to do. There's people like that in the world. They can't do nothing themselves, so they try to bring everybody else down to their can't-do-nothing level."

Elder Smitty was right, and both me and C.J. knew it. But him being right hadn't stopped Little Man from messing with C.J. and hadn't stopped him from dissing the church. So the thing was, in a way we were dealing at his level whether we wanted to or not.

I told C.J. to come on over to my house, and he said he just wanted to play awhile. He turned to the piano and

started playing "Amazing Grace." Reverend Loving, our minister, didn't like that song, and we never sang it in church or played it, but as C.J. sat at the piano playing, it sounded like the most beautiful song ever written. C.J. played for about five minutes straight, and then he was crying.

"Let him cry." Elder Smitty had come up to the piano and leaned against the walls. "Sometimes it takes tears to wash the pain that somebody like that young man can bring into your life."

I put my hand on C.J.'s shoulder as he played softly. "Don't let it bother you, man," I heard myself saying, knowing it didn't have any meaning.

"Old as I am, I've never learned to deal with people like him without bloodshed," Elder Smitty said. "You did real good, Jesse. We need to celebrate God and the joy in our lives and let these fools dance with Satan if they want."

I waited for C.J. to get himself together. It took a while. When he finally did, we left the church and walked toward home.

"Don't worry about it," I said. "We just have to outlast these dudes."

"He called me a faggot," C.J. said.

With SATAN!

"Hey, C.J., you go one-on-one with people like him and he's got to come out on top because there's nothing he cares for," I said. "Why would he want to hurt you, diss the church, diss Elder Smitty? The sucker is just evil."

"Man, I'm fifteen, I should be able to deal with dudes like him," C.J. said.

"You can deal with him," I said. "But not on his level. And he can't deal with you on yours. Word."

"Yeah, but I'm living in his world," C.J. said. "He's not living in mine."

"I don't have it all worked out in my head, but I know you're okay and we can be people together," I said. "We can't let fools drag us down to their level. If that's all they got, then that's all they got. We got something else."

ART THING

"I don't know if I got a level to deal on or not," C.J. said.

"You got talent, so you have a level to deal on," I said. "That's the word, chapter and verse. I got the art thing going on. You got the music thing going on, and that's important to me, because what you're doing makes me surer about what I'm doing. You see what I'm talking about?"

"You getting a little deep," C.J. said. "But it feels right."

MUSIC THING

STICKUP MAN DEFIANT

Mason Grier, the 19-year-old defendant, a member of the street gang called the Counts, made an obscene gesture at the end of his sentence procedure this Wednesday at Criminal Court in Manhattan. Ernest McKinnon, the state-appointed lawyer for the 19-year-old, promised an appeal of the 84-month sentence, which he denounced as "excessive."

"So what is this all about?" My father knew I had seen the article in the *Amsterdam News*. "Since when did the Counts become a street gang?"

"That's probably what Mason told them," I said. "He's trying to go down in a blaze of glory, like he's a superhero or something."

"He sure doesn't look like a superhero to me," my father said.

"He made the papers," I said.

"That's a superhero to you? Somebody who makes the papers?"

"I'm not saying that, Dad," I said, swinging my legs over the side of the bed. "What I'm saying is that guys like Mason jump on stuff like that as if they have done something wonderful. You can say it sucks, I can say it sucks, because he's in jail, but when you talk to them, they're acting as if it's big-time."

"I want you out of that club," my father said, taking the paper from me and folding it up. "You don't need to be no Count."

"Are you taking me out of the neighborhood, too?" I asked.

"Watch your mouth, boy." He raised a stubby finger in front of my face. "I brought you into this world and I can take you out of it!"

"Why don't you hit me?" I said. "Maybe you're as tough as Mason."

I didn't see the blow coming, and it caught me hard across the face. It stung my eye bad, and I started to bring my hands to my face, then stopped and just looked at him.

"That your best shot?" I asked. My right eye was blurring fast, but I could see he had his fist balled up, ready to hit me again.

He was yelling, something about how he hadn't raised a child to be going to prison. There were curses, too, and he kept pulling his fist back to hit me. I saw the anger in his face and it got me mad and we were both glaring at each other, with him standing over me, holding my bunched T-shirt in one hand and threatening me with the other.

The door opened, and I could hear Mom coming into the room. She pushed her way between us.

"Archie, please! Please!"

"You'd better teach that boy something before I kill him!" he said.

I could hear his breathing, short raspy breaths as he let my shirt go, giving me one final push before he stormed out of the room.

"Jesse, I heard you talking back to him, and what is . . ." She lifted my face and saw my eye was closed and turned away. She was crying as she leaned against my dresser.

The eye was throbbing and I couldn't get it open. The sound of the radio drifted in from the kitchen, and I imagined him sitting at the table, in his old man shirt, his neck still puffed from being mad. Mom took several deep breaths and started to say something but couldn't. Then she stood, sniffed, and rubbed her face in her palms.

"I think you should not have spoken . . ." She looked at my face again and told me to open my eye.

I tried, but it wouldn't open and she pulled the lid up. "Put your shirt on," she said, her voice cracking as she spoke. "We'd better have that eye looked at. Get dressed."

"It's all right," I answered.

"Jesse, this is already too hard for me." Mom's voice rose and cracked against the pale-blue walls of my room. "This is too hard for me! Please don't make it harder!"

She left, and I put my shirt on and a light jacket. The eye hurt like crazy, and I imagined myself going through life with one eye. Mom came back into the room and asked if I could see well enough to walk by myself.

"Do you want your father to help you?" she asked.

"What do you think?" I said.

It was pretty easy to see out of one eye, even though my good eye was a little closed, too. As

My Old Man

we went through the kitchen, I saw him sitting at the end of the table, just where I thought he would be, his eyes closed, his hand curled around a coffee cup.

We took a gypsy cab to Harlem Hospital and sat in the waiting room with some old people and a young guy who was nodding out on something. A doctor came out—he looked foreign, but black foreign—and shook the guy nodding out. The nodder opened his eyes, saw that it was a doctor standing in front of him, and started complaining about a pain in his back.

"I can't even tell you how bad it is," he slurred. "That's how bad it is."

The doctor told him he'd be with him in a minute. Mom stood and asked if there was an eye specialist around. "My son hurt his eye," she said, pointing toward me.

The doctor came over, pulled my eyelid open, and asked how it happened.

In the treatment room I had to lie on a bench until they could find someone to come look at my eye. The woman doctor who came asked me how old I was, and I told her.

She opened my eye and told me that the examination was going to hurt, and that I should try not to blink.

"I don't know why I say that, because I think you're either a blinker or not a blinker," she said as she shone a light into the eye. "It's a reflex."

I was a blinker. She had me look in as many directions

as I could, and then to try and follow the light.

Finally she announced that there was bleeding under the cornea but it probably wasn't permanently damaged. "You'll keep it covered for twenty-four hours, and keep yourself calm," she said. "Then have it checked again, just to make sure. No excitement, no basketball. You don't want too much pressure in your eyes. And don't read, even with the good eye, because the eyes work together even when you're not seeing out of one of them."

A nurse put a gauze patch over the eye and told me to keep my hands off it.

On the street the sunlight seemed a thousand times brighter than it had been before.

"Every day of our lives your father works for you," Mom said. "And every day of my life I pray for you and hope with all my heart that you'll be all right. That a cab won't hit you and a stray bullet won't hit you and that you'll get a decent education and that no gang will get you and no dope will find its way into you. And are you just too damned dumb to understand that? Are you just too dumb to understand that?"

"No."

"Then read the papers, Jesse," she said, "and figure out what it takes to raise a boy in this neighborhood."

The gypsy cabdriver saw Mom crying and made sure we had the money to pay the fare before he took us home. When we got to the stoop, where Calvin and Benny were sitting, I said I was going to hang out for a while. Mom said no, for me to come up and rest, and I said I didn't want to and sat on the stoop. Mom sat down next to Benny, which surprised the heck out of him.

"Hello, Mrs. Givens," Benny said. "I see you're hanging with the homeboys today."

"Just chillin'," Mom answered.

Nobody asked about my eye, or why Mom was crying, although I knew they were wondering. They didn't talk much either, and I knew they wouldn't as long as my mother was sitting there. When Calvin stood up and stretched and said he had to leave, Benny jumped up and stretched, too. A moment later they were both gone.

"You think it was something I said?" Mom asked.

I didn't answer. We sat there for a while longer, with me wondering what I would say to my father.

"When you were being examined, one of the policemen came over and asked me if I wanted to file an abuse report on your father," Mom said. "I said no, but my heart was really in my mouth as I was saying it. I know that if he had wanted to, he could have said that it didn't matter what I wanted, that he was supposed to file a police report any time a woman or a child is injured by a husband. But you know what I think convinced him not to file a report?"

"No, I don't," I said.

"I think he was impressed when I asked him not to make us just another family of abusive black people who didn't know how to treat each other," she said. "He was white, but he was wearing a wedding ring, so he probably had a family of his own."

"Yo, Mom, check it out—he hit me because he's scared about something he read in the newspaper," I said. "I didn't *do* anything. I can't be responsible for what he's thinking."

"Jesse, I'm sorry we're just humans," she said, her voice trembling. "You're free to blame us for not being perfect. Any time you want me to admit to it, just let me know. I'll stand up and bow my head for you. Okay?"

There were some things I didn't want to say to Mom. I didn't want her to know how confused I felt and how I wasn't sure of what the right thing was to do anymore. I didn't want to tell her that I hadn't known that Mason was nineteen, not seventeen like he had told us. Or how we were all so busy trying to be down with the program that we hadn't peeped him scamming us.

She stood and went into the building, and I felt stupid. My eye was hurting; I was mad at Dad for being afraid for me, even though in my heart I knew I was afraid, too. Where the heck were the easy answers?

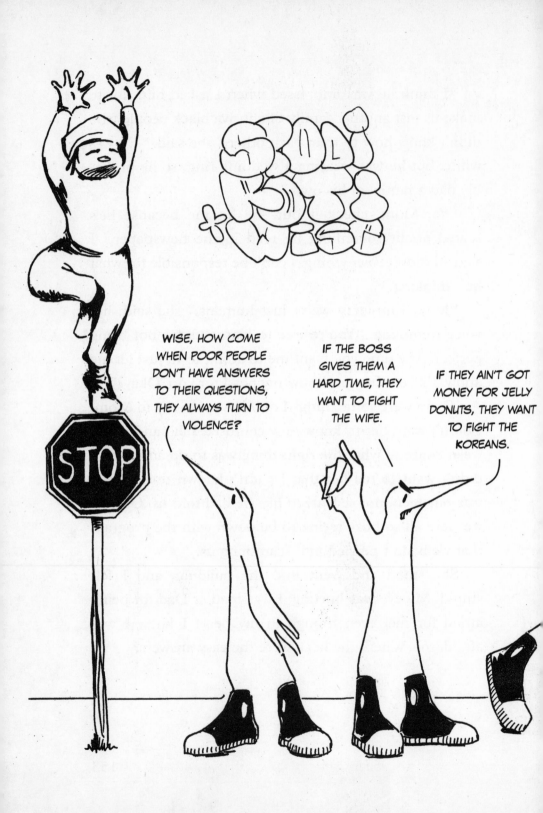

'CAUSE THEY AIN'T GOT NO AIR-PLANES TO DROP THE BOMBS, SPODI. AND THAT'S THE WORD.
IF SANTA CLAUS LOSE THEIR ADDRESS, THEY WANT TO BLOW UP CHRISTMAS.
IF THEY DON'T SEE A FUTURE FOR THEMSELVES, THEY WANT TO BEAT UP THE BOY CHILD. WHY THEY GOT TO BE BEATING ON THINGS?
STOP

16

Sunday. The eye was all right, just a little sore where the back of his nail had hit it, but I didn't like being anybody's punching bag, even if they thought they were right, which Dad did. I had read all the bits about black men not being able to express themselves and turning to violence to show their anger, but it didn't mean boo to me when it was me being hit.

Mom was all right, doing her neutral thing, and I hoped she was giving him a hard time when I wasn't around. He didn't say much to me, and I didn't say much to him, either.

"Are you going to church with us," Mom asked, standing in my doorway, "or are you mad with me, too?"

"Just don't feel like going," I said.

"I'm sorry you can't forgive us," she said. "So I guess we'll just have to wait until you do."

"I don't remember you hitting me," I said, looking at the hole in my sweat sock.

"My husband, your father, hit you, and I'm a hundred percent on his side."

"Even if he's wrong?"

"There's food in the refrigerator if you want breakfast."

I felt bad about not going to church. Maybe I was even working at staying mad. It wasn't that he had hit me the one time but the fact that if he wanted, he could do it again. We weren't that kind of family, and he had to hold up his end.

I took a shower, put on some clean underwear, and tried to figure out what I was going to do for the day. C.J.

PUNCHING BAG

hadn't called for a few days, and I thought about calling him or Tania. She had called again, saying she just wanted to say hello. She told me she had bought me a Chinese pen made of bamboo on 42nd Street. A guy down there was writing people's names in fancy letters, and she had bought one of his brushes, too.

I was thinking about doing someone's name in fancy letters. The Chinese artists who did them on the street were good, and fast. The way they controlled the brushes, never making mistakes, always keeping a steady pressure on the pad—that was way cool. I thought about writing Tania's name, maybe writing our names together. Tania and Jesse, or just our initials, J & T. I'd do it so that it looked like flowers coming out of a vase. I imagined how Tania would smile when she figured out it was our initials.

The phone rang, and it was Detective Rock.

"How are things going?" he asked.

"You have to work on Sundays, too?"

"I don't have to, really," he said. "But I figure if I don't work on Sundays sometimes, I end up working overtime during the week trying to clean up the mess I could have prevented on Sunday. How come you didn't go to church today?"

"You were at church today?"

"No, but when I called and you answered, I knew you weren't at church either."

"Sherlock Holmes."

"Jesse, I hear there's going to be a big confrontation between the Counts and the Diablos," Detective Rock said. "It's not the kind of thing I want to hear. The Counts are not that kind of a club. The Diablos are a bunch of guys who aren't going anywhere and don't have a thing to lose."

"That's why you called? To keep me from going down with the Diablos?" I asked.

"It doesn't sound real to me," Sidney said. "But sometimes I miss things. You know what I mean?"

"I guess I missed it too," I said.

"You know, you can still get most of the sermon if you hurry," Sidney said.

"Yeah, well, okay, I'm going to have to see about that," I said. "When are you getting there?"

"Jesse, you are a hard man," he said. "A hard man."

What I thought, after I had hung up, was that everybody was getting excited about the piece in the paper. Mason was running his mouth about his gang, and naturally the papers were printing it. Dad said that it used to be only the white papers that ran all the garbage news about black people; now it was the white and the black papers.

My eye was still sore and I tried to get my mad going again, but it was hard. I thought if I ever had a kid, I would never hit him. Even if he was wrong big-time, I would just sit down and talk to him. I figured if he was my kid, he would probably be boss anyway because I would be such a great parent.

My paints were in a box I kept on the dresser and I took them out, thinking I was going to practice painting Tania's name. But then I figured I didn't want to clean the brushes afterward, so I put them back into the box and called Tania's house. It excited me to think of us kissing or doing what Calvin called the grope-a-dope.

My sunglasses were cool, because everybody on the block knew I had hurt my eye and that's why I was wearing my shades. I also looked good in shades, so when I busted on down onto the stoop and White Clara was there, I could see her checking me out. She was probably interested but she wasn't really my type.

"So where you going?" she asked.

"Just checking out the happenings," I said. "You seen anybody around?"

"I'm around," she said.

"You think all I'm interested in is beautiful women?" I asked White Clara.

"Get out of here, boy." She sucked her teeth and looked away. "What's his name just passed by a little while ago—C.J."

I checked my watch and saw that church must be over. White Clara asked me if I wanted to use her cell to call him and I said yes.

C.J.'s mom answered the phone and, soon as she knew it was me, asked me how my eye was. I told her it was still painful, and she said she had wondered why I hadn't been in church. I covered the mouthpiece with my hand as a bus passed so she wouldn't know I was in the street. She said that C.J. had come home and gone right out again.

"That boy loves the streets more than he loves himself," she said.

"Will you ask him to give me a call when he gets home?"

She said that she would. I thought about going to a movie, checked my pockets, and found out that I didn't have any money. When I gave White Clara back her telephone, she asked me if I had a girlfriend.

"Sure," I said.

"Now that shows you how many desperate women there are in the world," she said.

Okay, she scored on that, but I remembered the line I had when I said did she think "all I'm interested in is beautiful women?" That was a line I was going to use again if I could remember it.

I went back inside. Upstairs, I searched my room for money. Nada. Into the clothes in my closet. Nada. I knew I could cop from Mom on a regular day, but now that she was showing large for Dad, she might want to make me go to him for money. I figured I'd get back with him, but I didn't want it to look like I was copping a humble, so I had to let a minute go by.

I was in my room when my folks got home.

The telephone rang. Mom got it and headed toward my room. I figured it was C.J. When Mom came to the door and said that it was Rise, I was surprised. She didn't say it funny or anything, just that Rise was on the phone.

"How was church?" I asked.

"Everybody asked about you," she said, smiling. "I told them your eye was bothering you and you were having trouble seeing the light."

"Thanks."

I got the phone and asked Rise what was up.

"Running late, my man," Rise said. "Look, there's going to be a meeting at Earl's Antiques tomorrow evening at six thirty. He's going to let us use his back room. We're going to be meeting with some of the Diablos to talk about turf. You know where Earl's is?"

"Yeah."

"Okay, try to be on time so we can show the Diablos we're correct even though it really ain't no big thing, just some mouth running. See you tomorrow."

My mouth was dry and my heart was pounding when I hung up the phone. I hadn't said anything about what Sidney had told me. Maybe it was just talk.

"What's Rise up to these days?" Mom asked.

"Running around," I said. "In a big hurry, as usual."

I was thinking about C.J. and how he liked to play the piano or organ. It's great to just sit and watch him at the keyboard, his eyes closed, his body swaying, all into his music. When nobody's around, he takes off his shoes and works the pedals with his bare feet. Sometimes I feel that way when my drawing is going good. It's as if when I'm putting marks on paper, even when I'm not drawing anything in particular, something is being created. Some space is being surrounded by a line and comes alive. Or a color, deep and rich, spreads itself across the page. Once in a while I surprise myself with a line or an image and I have to study the paper to see just what I've got. When that happens it feels so good. So good.

The brush I was holding felt heavy. I had dipped it into an almost empty jar of Nile green watercolor paint and brought it to the center of my drawing pad. My hand, fingers slightly extended the way I like to hold my brush, didn't move. I put it down. I was thinking too much. Images of Rise came up in my mind. Not the old Rise but the new one, with the lean and all the business he was getting into. I knew a meeting with the Diablos couldn't be a good thing. I wasn't down for no gang-banging, but it was as if we were being sucked into it.

The point was that I needed to do something to pull back. The easy thing was to start dropping dimes. I didn't want to call Sidney, but I thought I might deal with my father. Get his butt upset enough and he would either kill me to keep me safe or come up with something. But that meant I had to rat out Rise and look like I was just punk-ing out. In a way I didn't mind backing down or looking like a punk—I just didn't want to be the first to take the step.

Mom called through the door, asking if I wanted any-thing to eat. I said no.

"You want some eggs?" she asked.

"No."

Her head appeared in the doorway. "Tuna on toast?"

I said okay and she thanked me with a smile.

What was I going to do? I hadn't said that I would meet Rise at the store, but I hadn't told him I wouldn't either. When he was talking, I was listening to him and searching for something to say back. I knew what C.J. meant at the church. I didn't want to show lame all the time, but I didn't know what style I should be wearing.

Dad and Mom and Sidney had that distant thing

going on. THE RIGHT THING FOR YOU TO DO IS . . . STAY AWAY FROM THE MEETING . . . HIDE UNDER THE BED . . . LISTEN TO YOUR PARENTS. . . . WHAT WOULD JESUS DO?

But I was right in the middle of the joint, and it wasn't a hundred percent clear what the action was. If I started dropping dimes and nothing was shaking, I would really look like a punk.

I narrowed my people-to-talk-to list down to Tania and C.J. Tania would probably have wanted to go kick the crap out of the Diablos, so she slipped off the list. Mom brought in the tuna sandwich just as I was picking up the phone to call C.J.

"That was quick," I said.

"And my fingers never left my hands," she said. "Don't leave the crumbs in your room. Roaches love tuna on toast."

The phone rang five times and I was just ready to hang up when C.J. answered. I asked him if he had heard there was a meeting tomorrow night.

"Yeah, I'll see you there," he said, sounding like he wanted to get off the phone.

"You going?"

"Yeah, Benny called me. He said he couldn't make it but Calvin and Gun are going," C.J. said.

"Yo, man, I got a call from Sidney, and he said he heard there was going to be a throwdown between the

Counts and the Diablos," I said. "I don't know how we're getting involved in this thing. They got guns and doing drive-bys and stuff."

"Well, that's the way it goes," C.J.'s voice was almost a whisper.

"You're not alone?"

"I'm alone," he said.

"Why you talking so low?"

"It's the way I feel."

"If this thing is going to be a fight or something, why you going?" I asked. "You're no banger."

"I just decided I can't be limping all my life," C.J. said.

"Is this about that thing in the church with Little Man?" I asked. "Because he's the one that's jive, not you."

"Maybe it's about who I am," C.J. said. "Somewhere along the way you got to decide. It's like, there comes a time and you got to put a name on things. I can't be hiding in church all my life."

"Why not? It's what you do, isn't it?" I said. "Not the hiding part but the being in church. All of a sudden you don't think that's cool?"

"It's cool, but there's more stuff out there that we got to deal with," he said. "You know, there's a time for every purpose, man. So this is my time to check out the meeting. You coming?"

"I don't know," I said. "If I don't come, will you think I'm weak?"

"You know, Jesse, a guy once said to me that you don't know if you can really get into some music unless you sit down and do it. You can't look at the notes on paper and say, 'Hey, it's easy.' We here talking about getting into life and I don't even know if I got the heart for the part," C.J. said. "You see where I'm coming from?"

"I guess so," I said. "Or can I catch a maybe?"

"You got the maybe," C.J. said.

"C.J., look, if something does go down, maybe we can look out for each other," I said.

"We'll see," C.J. answered.

What I had hoped for was C.J. to feel the same way that I did. We would both say no way and that would have been the whole game, with us backing each other up. I didn't think I was going to go, but I was looking for somebody to help me say the words.

I took a bite out of the tuna sandwich, but I wasn't in the mood for it and put it up. I got out the book I was doing on Rise and laid out some pictures I had of him on my bed.

I thought about what other pictures I could use instead of just photos of Rise and me and his family. I remembered a time when we were small—Rise was seven so I must have been five—and were on a church picnic to Van Cortlandt Park. We all had to wear badges with our names on them. One kid had a badge that read Junior, and a counselor asked him what his real name was. It was Richard, the same as his father's name. Rise took the kid's badge and wore it, and the kid was crying. The counselor made him give it back, and Rise made his own badge that said Junior because he wanted to have one that said he had a father.

The real badge was square, but I drew it round and then didn't have enough room to write the whole word *junior*, so it came out JUNIor. I figured I would redo it later and put the pad away.

I had come up with an answer to what I should do. I just hoped that he was home.

My hands were sweaty and I wiped them on my pants legs as I dialed. The phone rang twice and Rise picked up.

"Look, Rise, I got a call from Rock and he thinks the Diablos are planning some kind of confrontation." I let the words tumble from my lips in a rush because I needed to get them out quickly. "And if anything goes down, you're going to be the one they're going to try to waste."

"Ain't no big thing," Rise said. "Me, the prophet Enoch, and the prophet Elijah go walking hand in hand. They're the Saints and I'm the Man. Nothing to it, schoolboy."

"You're not worried that they might try something?" I asked.

"Chill, bro," Rise said. "Sidney don't know everything. He just wants to pretend he does. That's his job. When's the last time anyone arranged a gangbang and ran it by the po-lice?"

"Yeah, I guess."

"See you tomorrow, man."

The phone clicked and went dead. My eye started hurting again, and I switched off the light and lay across the bed.

In my head I ran the tape of the telephone conversation. Rise hadn't sounded scared at all, not even nervous. I thought about how C.J. had sounded and how I felt inside. Then I had another thought. Maybe it wasn't that Rise was sure that nothing would happen at the meeting. Maybe he just wasn't afraid of dying.

20

I walked downtown, realizing how nervous I was as my stomach started cramping. My head was heading for the meeting, but my feet were having other ideas. Earl's window was piled high with leftover stuff from life along Malcolm X Boulevard. There were old lamps with colored globe shades, photographs of black boxers who didn't look that tough, and small piles of gold and silver costume jewelry. A few blocks up was Striver's Row, still pretending it was cool, still pimping on its Harlem Renaissance props. The truth was that the whole neighborhood was a little bit of a hustle. Some of the hustle was hardworking folks chasing their behind-closed-doors dreams. Others were the people who had blown their dreams and were just chasing whatever life they could get at.

Earl would give you a couple of dollars for a radio in good condition, or a quarter for a flashlight that still worked. Once in a while something valuable would find its way into his store. Earl knew everybody and he was decent to them all, which is why I liked him.

"You always have to add seventy-five cents to the price of the crack to cut the deal," Earl said.

Earl made his money mostly from white antiques dealers who came to Harlem looking for bargains. They paid good money for costume jewelry, old photographs, pieces of people's lives that had died or had just got too tired to hang on to anymore.

Earl came to our church from time to time. Sister Essie called him a red-number Christian because he came to church only when the number on the calendar was red, showing that it was a holiday like Christmas or Easter.

I nodded and asked if Rise was there, and Earl pointed toward the back room.

"Don't you go to that church off 145th Street?" he asked, knowing that I did.

"Yeah, sometimes," I said, trying to make it sound more casual than I felt inside.

Earl's back room was a surprise. The front of the store was piled high with junk, but the back was clean and neat. Rise, C.J., Gun, and some girl I had never seen before were sitting around an enamel kitchen table. There was an old record player against one wall and a couch against the other. On the wall was a picture of Malcolm X over an advertisement for Ray's Barber Shop.

171

C.J. avoided looking at me. Gun put his fist up and we brushed knuckles lightly.

"Yo, Jesse, this is my old lady." Rise pointed to the girl. She was too young for him. He closed his eyes for a moment, as if he was trying to remember something. Then opened them and nudged the girl. "Uh, go on and tell him your name, baby."

"Rise, you know my name!" the girl said, embarrassed.

"Yeah, but I want you to tell him," Rise said.

"It's Junice," the girl said.

"Yeah, Jesse here is writing my life up," Rise went on. "I've been telling him there's three important times in a man's life. The first was when he's born. That's about the circumstances he got going for him. Then when he dies. That's about what he'd done with his days. But there's one minute in his life where he makes the big D to take over his life. That's what most people don't do, take charge of their lives. Ain't that right, Jesse?"

"Yeah, I guess that's right," I said.

"So what's going down with the Diablos?" Gun cut to the chase.

"You know—and Jesse can back me up on this—the Diablos have been checking out their press, and now they're thinking they can blow themselves up huge if they get the right coverage." Rise had slipped out of his OG voice and was talking like he did before he started hanging uptown. "Their crew got to the point where they're putting all their business in the street. They got shorties running around talking about how the Diablos did this and how they did that.

"Now, if shorties are running up and down the Avenue laying out your thing, you know the police and everybody else is checking you out too. Ain't that right, Jesse?"

"Yeah."

"That's why Jesse and Gun were worried about what they were going to be doing," Rise went on. "It's like 'Hey, the revolution is going to be on television tonight at eight thirty—bring your own piece.' You know what I mean?"

"They're supposed to be revolutionaries?" Junice asked.

"Naw, I'm talking history," Rise said. "The Counts are some heavy dudes. They dig where I'm coming from. So what I'm saying is that we got to walk away from the Diablos and let them do their little gang thing on their own turf and deal with whatever business they got to be dealing with away from us. You see what I'm saying?"

"We got to fight them to put them out of the hood?" C.J. asked.

"No, man, we just got to walk away from their game, away from their press conferences, and be who we are in our own quiet way."

Junice asked Rise if the Diablos really had press

conferences, and he gave her a look and started explaining again how they put their business in the streets so they might as well call the television reporters down and run their whole game for the public.

What I was thinking was that it was cool to stay away from the Diablos, but I still didn't have the whole 411 because the way Rise was running it down, the words didn't sound like they fit the melody. A year before, Rise had been just an ordinary dude; now he was sounding like Moses coming down from the mountainside, passing out commandments, signing autographs, and blowing kisses to his fans.

He ran his mouth some more about how we were more mature than the Diablos, and I could see C.J. and Gun relaxing. Gun was even bad-mouthing Calvin and Benny for not making the meeting.

"They're reading the same press as the Diablos," Rise said.

I was feeling better too. Before I had come into Earl's, I was so uptight I couldn't think. Now the pain in my stomach was easing up and I was trying to figure out what was coming next.

Something came to me saying that the set was too easy. And when Rise was checking his watch and wondering aloud what had happened to the Diablos, it didn't feel right. Gun wondered how come they were late.

"They ain't got their handle down," Rise said.

"Mostly they're young dudes with more rep than weight."

"So all we're going to do is chill, right?" C.J. was saying.

"And stay beautiful," Rise said, turning to the girl. "Ain't that right . . . baby?"

"Junice!" The girl pushed Rise playfully.

"So Jesse's writing about you taking charge of your life?" Gun asked.

"Yeah, I'm telling him what it's about, and he's putting it all down in words and bringing it to life on the page. He's like my P. Diddy, orchestrating my thing and bringing out the best in me. And let me explain that the brother's words and images are just righteous. Righteous!"

"Jesse is good," C.J. said.

"Maybe we can have a party when the book is done, and me and him can sign copies like the white folks do," Rise said.

Earl came into the back room and asked us how much longer we were going to be because he wanted to go and get something to eat. Rise said our business was finished and we just had to wrap things up a bit.

"Two minutes, Earl."

Earl nodded. He had eyeballed the whole room and sniffed to see if there was any weed in the air. Everything was cool, and I was glad the meeting was ending.

"So we're not going to wait for the Diablos?" I asked.

"They ran their mouths about me not being late, and it's after seven now. The lames are gaming, so we might as well check the breeze. I'm going to try to get cell phones for all the Counts." Rise stood up. "That way we can stay in touch easier. We can still have our meetings once a month."

"You can get me a phone too," Junice said as we started out the door.

Rise flagged down a gypsy cab and asked if any of us needed to be dropped off. Gun went with him, and me and C.J. started walking uptown.

"So what you think?" C.J. asked.

Bob Marley's voice came out of a loudspeaker mounted over a small incense store. He was singing "No Woman No Cry," and it sounded as good as it always did. "Rise is so many people," I said. "One minute he's talking about the Diablos going big-time and the next he's getting us all cell phones so we can stay in touch. I guess it's all right."

"Everybody is more than one person," C.J. said.

"What's that mean?"

"You just said that," C.J. came back. "You said that Rise is so many people."

"I know what I said," I answered. "I said that because he keeps changing the direction he's coming from. But what did you mean when you said it?"

"Everybody changes the direction they're coming

176

from," C.J. said. "I change the
direction I'm coming from all
the time."

"I don't change my
direction," I said.

"That's because
you're not as smart
as me," C.J.
said.
"You
know I'm a
genius, right?"

"Yeah, you
probably are,
man." I could tell
that C.J. was as relieved as I was that nothing had happened. We started kidding with each other as we walked
uptown. C.J. stopped to buy a soft-shell crab on a bun
from a wide-faced old woman who was mostly bald and
had a wig on that had slid toward the back of her head.

"What you want on it?" she asked. "All I got is hot
sauce."

"Then why you ask me what I want on it?" C.J. asked.

"Don't play with me, boy." The woman pushed a
stubby finger under C.J.'s nose. "I don't need your two
dollars that bad."

C.J. started to protest that the sign read $1.75 when

we heard the first sirens. People on the street turned to look, saw that the emergency vehicles were passing where we were, and went on with whatever they were doing. I looked and saw that there were three regular police cars and two unmarked cars with blue lights on top. They were all headed uptown.

"It's a stickup," C.J. said. "The store owner pushed the silent alarm and the cops are trying to catch the stickup dudes in the store."

"I think it's a liquor-store stickup because they're the only ones that pay off the police," I said. "That's why the cars are hustling uptown. Either a liquor store or a fast-food place. Probably a fast-food place, because the liquor stores all have that bulletproof glass and you can't get to the money."

"You can if you take a hostage," C.J. said.

We got to 144th Street, and we saw there were about nine police cars, some emergency vehicles, and cops all over the place. We asked a man what happened and he said he didn't know. A girl, about ten, heard us ask and came over right away.

"There was some shooting and people was running all over 144th Street. One guy got shot in the stomach, and he was holding his stomach and hollering, 'I'm shot! I'm shot!' and he didn't even need to be hollering that because you could see his butt was shot. They were shooting people from their cars, and the people they were shooting at was shooting back at them. A bullet just missed me!"

"You were right there?" C.J. asked.

"Not at first, but I ran up the block to see what was going on because my cousin lives on that block—in 216—and I went up to her house on the first floor, and we were all looking out the window and we could see them shooting. One of them had an Uzi, and he hit a pregnant lady in her foot and she was screaming. It was terrible."

"Anybody get hurt bad?" I asked.

"You know the one I said got shot in the stomach?"

"Yeah."

"I think he was dead, because he was sitting on the sidewalk and not even moving and his hand was like this across his lap and his head was back like this and one leg was kind of up but it wasn't moving and my cousin said he looked like he was dead."

The police were moving everybody off the street, and C.J. said that we had better get home before our parents heard about it.

"No way we get home that fast," I said. "Look, channel two is already here."

I got home and my parents

I'M SHOT!
I'M SHOT!

were watching television. Dad looked at the clock on the mantel but he didn't say anything.

"Night, folks," I said.

Mom said good night and Dad kind of grunted. It was good to be talking again.

21

I went to sleep thinking about Tania. It was funny how she kept showing up in my thoughts even though I was so nervous when I was around her. At first I tried to keep my thoughts on drawing her and away from sex, but after a while I just gave in and wondered about what it would be like to be with her. I wasn't really worried about it, because I didn't think we were going to get married or anything super serious, but I didn't want her to think I was a goofus, either. Thinking about Tania led me into thinking about C.J. He and Tania were the ones I wanted to be with. C.J. because he was easy and we had the art thing going on, and Tania because she was a girl. I kept remembering the way she looked at me when she told me that she was going to tell Rise that we had done it. Yikes. *Yes, Mami, you definitely got it going on.*

When Mom woke me, I thought it was morning. But when she put her arms around me and started whispering something about Sidney, I knew something was crazy wrong.

"Remember, you don't have to say anything to him or to the police," she whispered in my ear. She was in her bathrobe. Her arms were around me, holding me close.

"What's up?"

"That detective is here," she said. "Sidney."

"What's up?" I asked again.

"He said he wants to talk to you, and it's something serious," she said, still half whispering. "Are you awake enough to hear me?"

"Yeah."

"Some boys were shot on 144th Street," she said. "Two died and one is in bad condition. They want to question you about it."

"I wasn't on 144th Street," I said. "Me and C.J. passed it on the way home and saw the police cars and everything, but that's about it. They weren't even letting people walk down the block."

"Your father thinks we should get a lawyer anyway," Mom said.

"What for? I didn't do anything," I said.

"No one is accusing you of doing anything," Mom answered, patting me on the shoulder. "But we're your parents, and we're a little . . ." She was holding on, trying not to cry.

"Yo, Mom, you don't have anything to worry about,"

I said. "I didn't do anything. When me and C.J. came home, we saw the police cars tearing up the streets. When we got to 144th we saw all the commotion. No way we were involved in it."

The door opened and Dad came in.

"What he say?" Dad stood in front of the door. He looked enormous.

"He said that he and C.J. were walking home and just saw the commotion when they passed 144th Street," Mom answered. "Did you call Joe Charles?"

"Yeah. He said not to say anything," Dad said. "Look, Jesse, you got to go downtown with Sidney. But don't say nothing to him. Nothing. If he ask you what day it is, don't say nothing! Joe's on his way."

"You understand that, Jesse?" Mom asked. "It's not about whether you did anything or not. It's that we're dealing with the system, and we have to understand their rules. If you don't say anything until Joe Charles talks to you, you're going to be better off. You have to trust us on this one, baby."

She was crying. Tears were running down her face, and she was breathing hard, as if she was having an asthma attack or something. I knew I hadn't done anything, but I was getting scared.

"Yeah, okay. I won't say anything."

"Get dressed," she said. "We're going down to the precinct with you."

She left the room to get dressed, and Dad sat on the bed. His face looked puffy, and I knew he was scared, too. I put on my pants and a T-shirt, slipped into my sneakers, and started to the bathroom. Dad came out with me. On the way, I saw Sidney sitting at the kitchen table. He looked exhausted, and I felt a little sorry for him.

"I understand you told him not to speak to me." Sidney looked tired as he spoke to my father. "And that's fine with me. But he has to ride in the car with me, because I'm bringing him in on official police business."

"Don't say anything to him," Dad said, his voice loud and aggressive. "If he asks you how you feel, don't even answer!"

I looked at Sidney and he looked cool with it.

In the bathroom I looked at myself in the mirror as I peed. I wasn't worried or anything, but I decided to be sure not to speak to Sidney.

We went downstairs, and I saw there was his car plus a police car and a police emergency vehicle in front of the house. Sidney raised his hand and signaled one of the officers leaning against the car that everything was all right. I got into the back of his old Taurus. As soon as the door closed, I wanted to talk to him, to tell him I hadn't done anything.

"Your folks are looking for a ride," Sidney said. "Let me get them something."

He got out of the car and asked Dad if he wanted a ride in the police car. I could see Dad shake his head no and start looking for a cab. Sidney got back into the car with me.

"As far as I can tell, there were two meetings called tonight," he said, looking at me in the rearview mirror. "You guys were down at Earl's. C.J. told me and so did Gun."

"I didn't know anything about two meetings," I said, wondering why I was talking after promising Mom and Dad I wouldn't. "We just sat around and talked. It was me, C.J., Rise, Gun, and a girl. I don't remember her name right now, but Earl, the guy who owns the shop, saw us there and everything."

"Junice."

"That's right," I said. "And I don't remember when we left, but I know we were walking up Lenox Avenue— not all of us—"

"You and C.J.," Sidney said. "By the time you guys left Earl's it was all over."

"Then how come I'm getting arrested?"

"You're not arrested," Sidney said. "You're being picked up on suspicion of being involved in the setup. But I think you guys were the ones really being set up."

"I shouldn't talk to you, man, but what you talking about?"

"I won't ask you any questions," Sidney said. "But

there were apparently two meetings set up. The Counts, at least the ones who showed up, met at Earl's. The Diablos were sent to an address on 144th Street. The Diablos said it was a meeting of the top six Diablos and the top six Counts. It was supposed to be a discussion of territory. Who controlled which blocks. And a reporter from the *Amsterdam News* was going to mediate the whole thing."

"Get out of here!"

"Somebody had figured the Diablos would go for that," Sidney said.

What had Rise said? That the Diablos just wanted their names in the papers. I knew I had better keep my mouth shut.

"Mom said two people were killed," I said. "Is that true?"

"Two gone, one on the way," Sidney said. "It's serious."

The cars in front of the precinct were parked facing the building, and Sidney eased his car between two black-and-white police vehicles. On the sidewalk two cops were trying to get a drunk up the stairs and into the station house.

The precinct on 135th Street was always busy. Sidney brought me in and said something to the desk sergeant. The sergeant asked me if I needed anything to eat, and I said no. Then Sidney took me into a back room. C.J. was sitting on a couch with his mother and a man I didn't know.

C.J. was looking miserable, as if he had just been caught doing something big-time, and that made me smile a little.

"Yo, C.J., you look like a hood," I said.

"This is very serious, Jesse," C.J.'s mom said. "Some children have been killed."

"They got Gun, Rise, and that girl in another part of the precinct," C.J. said in a hoarse whisper.

I knew it was serious. C.J.'s mom didn't want him here waiting to see what was going on. This was the kind of thing you read about in the paper, something that happened to somebody else.

There was a voice in my head that kept repeating that me and C.J. didn't have anything to worry about, but there was nothing in the room except worry.

Mom and Dad came in. The first thing that came out of Dad's mouth was whether or not I had said anything to Sidney.

"I just asked him what happened," I said.

C.J.'s mom introduced the man they were with as her brother, and he and Dad shook hands. Then Dad came over and put his arm around me.

There was a low hum from the soda machine against the wall. On the right side of the machine, next to the coin slot, were two red lights and a green light. There was an automatic coffee machine on the table next to the couch we were sitting on, but the cord was unplugged. Three empty Styrofoam cups were lying in front of it. I wondered how many people had sat on the couch during the day looking at those cups.

The walls were gray on the bottom and yellow on top. The gray paint looked okay, but the yellow on top was in bad condition.

"I wonder why just the yellow paint is peeling," I said. I didn't know why I said it, or why I had even noticed it.

Mom looked at it and smiled, started to say something, and then looked away.

I thought about what C.J.'s mom had said, that some children had been killed, and wondered where their parents were and what they were doing. Were they holding each other and crying? Were they asking the police what had happened? And how about the kid who wasn't dead?

I thought about him in a hospital room somewhere, trying to keep his heart going, maybe trying to breathe, to stay alive.

The whole scene was just so messed up. It could have been me or C.J. just as easy as it had been the Diablos. The colors didn't matter. Bullets didn't know nothing about good guys and bad guys.

It was another fifteen minutes before Joe Charles came in. He was wearing jeans and a light jacket. He asked who everybody was and got introduced all around.

C.J.'s mom asked if she needed to call a lawyer. Mr. Charles said that he had spoken with Sidney and there didn't seem to be much of a problem.

"What they're thinking is that the boys were being used to provide an alibi," Mr. Charles said. "Still, we don't want to get involved in answering a lot of questions. I've known Sidney a long time, and he's a good man, but he's not the only one involved in this case. When this hits the papers tomorrow, I know the mayor's office is going to be involved. Three young men killed in a single night is just terrible, but—"

"The other one didn't make it?" Mom's voice was almost a shriek.

"No," Mr. Charles said. "All three of them are gone."

Mom started crying really hard and Dad took his arm from around me and turned to her. But the way Mom was crying, her body moving as she sobbed, it held him back. He turned toward the middle of the room, like he didn't know what to do, and I could see how upset he was. Joe Charles knelt down in front of Mom and held her hands.

It was terrible to see Mom crying like that, and to know why she was crying.

The whole room was filled with the sounds she made—almost grunting sounds—as if she was in a lot of pain. For a long time it was just those sounds and the humming of the soda machine, and then her breathing and the humming. I wanted to go over to the machine and pull out the cord. I didn't.

"Jesse talked to that detective," Dad said. "I don't know what all he said but he talked to him even though we told him not to say anything."

"It's okay. Ninety-nine percent of people want to present their side of the issue," Mr. Charles said. "If they pursue this end of the deal, it's going to be in the direction of a conspiracy charge, and that won't happen."

"What deal?" C.J.'s mom's voice was flat and hard.

"What they're looking at is the possibility of a drug war between an out-of-town drug group—gang, cartel, what have you—and the Diablos. All the victims were Diablos. A bunch of wild kids standing off against a sophisticated group with the weapons and the muscle to mess them up."

"You hear that, boy?" C.J.'s uncle gave him a mean look. "This is what I've got to be taking time off from work to deal with!"

"What's going to happen next?" Mom's head was down.

"They're going to let everybody go home tonight," Mr. Charles said. "The police uptown have made some arrests, but it won't have anything to do with these kids. If the police call you and ask you questions, call me, just to be on the safe side. I don't think anybody has anything

190

to worry about except if the mayor's office starts putting pressure on these cops to make a lot of quick arrests."

"They need to stay away from each other?" C.J.'s mom asked.

"No, they haven't done anything," Mr. Charles said. "They can just go on and live their normal lives. They need to know that somebody they both know, at least according to Sidney, a Rise Davis, is under suspicion and his name was mentioned when they made arrests uptown. And the most important thing they need to know is that even though they are completely innocent, and I'm sure they are, this is a serious issue. We're talking homicides here. This is nothing to brag about, nothing to take lightly."

"They need to stay away from Rise," Dad said.

"I would," Mr. Charles said. "If he calls, I'd be busy, and I think you need to let him know that you want to stay away from him. Don't be shy about it."

Sidney came in and said we could go. He said that he would let us know if anything developed, and would let Mr. Charles know, too.

When we got home, the sky was gray with streaks of sunlight breaking through. Mom wanted us to pray together, and I could see Dad didn't want to—he wanted to be tough because that's what he understood. I hadn't known that about him before, because he didn't act that way usually.

We sat together in the living room and Mom prayed. She got real emotional, crying and everything. She even prayed for the families of the Diablos who were shot. I got emotional too.

My drawing pad was on the dresser. I threw it on the bed and took my shirt off. Mom came in and gave me a hug, laying her head on my shoulder.

"You okay?" I asked.

"Yes," she said, looking up at me and smiling. She sounded sure, and that made me feel better. I realized that's why she had come into the room.

When she left, I lay across the bed and started looking at the drawings I had done of Rise. I stopped at one drawing—I had tried to have him looking out of the page at me—and tried to read the face I had drawn. This wasn't the Rise I had grown up with, the one who had put his arm against mine as we mingled our blood. That Rise had died somewhere in the past year, perhaps even the past few weeks. The Rise I knew could not have set anyone up to be shot, to be killed.

What had happened, what I felt, was that the old Rise, the Rise with clear, wise eyes and an easy grin, had crossed over into a different landscape and what we were doing, Rise and me, was trying to create someone new. The new Rise would be able to look at people and see ways to make himself important, and to believe the things he needed to believe to walk the streets he walked. I wasn't angry with Rise, although something told me I should be. But I didn't understand him anymore.

I picked up the sketchbook and turned to a blank page and started drawing Rise again. I wanted to draw the old Rise, the one that I had trusted and loved. My memory of him didn't work, so I took down one of the photographs I had stuck in the corners of my mirror.

After a while there were marks on paper, but the image never came.

The shootings made the paper the next day, and everybody on the block already knew I had been picked up. People I didn't even know were asking me questions. It made me mad to think that my friends, kids and grownups who thought I was a nice guy one day, could think the next day I was shooting people in the streets. And in a way they wanted me to be involved in the shooting simply because it made it all more exciting for them. I asked White Clara if she didn't feel sorry for the Diablos who had been shot, and she shrugged.

"How you going to shed tears for somebody who wants to be in that life, yo?"

When I spoke to C.J., he told me that his moms was trying to blame it on jazz.

"She said if you give the devil a crack, he'll slide on in," C.J. said.

"So what did you say?"

"I told her if I was studying music like I wanted, I probably wouldn't have time for gangs and stuff."

"She go for that?" I asked.

"She's thinking about it," C.J. said, smiling.

Sidney said that there had been some arrests made in the shootings. Some guys Rise had been dealing with uptown were picked up and charged, but he didn't know if they could make anything stick. The story was in the papers for another day or two, and then there was a big scandal with a ballplayer being accused of a hit-and-run accident and covering it up in Los Angeles, and the paper was full of that and people began to forget about the shootings. But then it all came back, like something that had been there all along, just not finished.

Rise called. I hadn't spoken to him since the meeting at Earl's. He told me that he had been held at Rikers for a week and now was out.

"I'm moving out of the city," he said. "Got to say good-bye to all my homeys and look for some greener pastures. This shooting thing messed me around a lot. I realized it just wasn't me to have to be ducking and watching my back."

What about the guys who were killed?

"I sure don't need that life," I said.

"Like my grandfather says, 'There's a time to gather stones,'" Rise said. "I'll just slip and slide for a while and gather a few stones until I see what's going down. You know what I mean?"

No, I didn't.

I asked him what he was going to do, and he said he was going to Florida, some place called Liberty City in Miami.

"Your folks okay with you splitting to Miami?"

"Yeah, I guess," Rise said. "Everybody knows this scene ain't making it."

"Yo, Rise, you don't sound like you used to," I said.

"I know, bro. That's why I got to get into business someplace where the weather fits my mood," he said, stretching out mood like it was cool or something. He said he was going to stop by in a day or two to say so long to all the fellows.

196

"Yeah, I'll take my life story down to Miami with me, let them know who I am," he said. "You know you can publish your own book if you got the cash."

Yeah.

When Rise hung up, I felt tired. I didn't want to give him the pictures I had drawn, and I didn't want to keep working on the book. I thought that if he just left and I kept them, there might come a time when it all came together for me and I would understand just who he was. Maybe.

We had another week until school started. When I thought of that, I also thought about the guys who were killed on 144th Street. I wondered if they would have gone back to school.

When Rise called to say he was leaving New York to live with relatives in Miami, he sounded really depressed.

"I'm going to miss you, bro." His voice cracked. "Guess we got to give it some time before we hook up again."

"Yeah, I guess."

"Look, I'll be pulling out at noon," he said. "Maybe you can give me a wave for old times' sake."

"Yeah, I'll see you then," I said.

I told myself again that I was just letting Rise go and moving on with my life. I took out the book I was doing and thumbed through it, looking at the photographs and the pictures I had drawn, thinking how hard it was going to be to say good-bye. Some of the drawings were good, really good. But after everything had went down the way

197

it had, I wasn't sure which ones looked like Rise and which were just images from my memory. I didn't know if I liked it, and I wondered if Rise would after some time had passed. Then, suddenly, it came to me—the book was coming out wrong, and I knew why it was wrong. It was so clear that I felt myself getting excited, and I knew I would have to explain it carefully to Rise.

When I got to the stoop, Benny was already there running his mouth to C.J. Rise had called them both. I was a little nervous, but I was ready to say good-bye to Rise and to tell him that he was the one who had to finish the book, not me. He had to get his own images together and his own style and decide who he wanted to be. It didn't matter if he couldn't draw well, because only he knew what the person he wanted to be would look like. I knew who I wanted him to be and so did a lot of other people, but that wasn't good enough.

I was excited and only half listening to what Benny was talking about as I tried to get my words together. I was going to give Rise the book with all my drawings and explain how he was the only person in the world who could finish it, and that would be my last gift to him. I could imagine him understanding where I was coming from and feeling the love I was showing him.

I had the book with the loose pages inside the cover when the white limo pulled up to the curb.

"Yo, don't tell me my man got a limo to go to the airport!" Benny said. "He's stepping in style!"

Sure enough, when the chauffeur came around and opened the door, who came out but Rise. He was dressed down in a gray suit with a pink shirt and some bad patent leather shoes. He could have been an entertainer.

Rise crossed his arms against his chest and leaned against the car so everybody could scope how fine he looked.

"Yo, my peeps!" he said, holding up his hands with his fingers spread apart. "Peace and salutations to the hood. Peace and salutations to the good. May the hood and the good always walk together!"

"You own that stretch?" Benny asked, pointing to the car.

Rise didn't answer. He saw me on the top of the steps and pointed toward me with two fingers. I didn't know what to do, to turn away from him or to go and shake his hand one last time as I said good-bye. I didn't have to make up my mind.

"Yo, Rise!"

We turned and saw Little Man standing on the sidewalk. He had his hand in a brown paper bag. When he took it out there was only a second between seeing the glint of the metal and hearing the *pop! pop!* of the bullets being fired at Rise.

We were running again, dodging into buildings, running

into hallways, screaming. Up and down the block old women were slamming windows shut and moving away from them, men were looking for something solid to get behind, kids were lying flat against the concrete sidewalk, covering their heads.

It was over in a minute. People were shouting something about Little Man and pointing down the street. A girl was screaming. Another one was crying.

Then I saw Rise. He was lying in the street at the back of the limo. He was reaching up as if he was trying to reach the bumper. I ran over to him and knelt down in the street. There was blood on his shirt, and his chest was heaving.

"Oh, Jesse!" he said. "Oh, man, it's so bad! It's so bad! Jess, don't let me go, man. Don't let me go!"

"You'll be okay," I said, getting down on my knees next to him. "Hang on, man."

"I don't think so," he said. "I don't think so. Yo, man, I'm crazy scared. Yo, call somebody!" He took my hand and squeezed it for a moment. Then he was calling my name over and over and his eyes were searching my face. They looked so wild and desperate.

"Yo, Jesse. I'm scared, man. I'm so scared!"

I was crying and trying to hold on to him and looking around hoping somebody would come and do something. I held Rise close to my chest and we were crying together. And then he went limp in my arms.

Precious Lord, take my hand
Lead me on, let me stand
Lord, I am so tired
Yes, I'm weak
And yes, I'm worn . . .

"The Lord giveth and the Lord taketh away. Blessed be the name of the Lord, and blessed be those who live in the righteousness that he has bestowed upon us. Brothers and sisters, truly it is a sorrowful thing for us to gather here in yet another going-home ceremony for a young man not yet reached his prime. We will miss Rise Davis and mourn his passing. But we are assured today that our God is a living God and a forgiving God and a God willing to take into His loving arms all those who have laid their heads down for that final and eternal rest.

"The book of life does not close after one page or one chapter. It goes on and on, and we who are left must continue the wonderful story by writing, not just with our pens, but with the moving pen of our daily lives." Pastor Loving wiped the sweat from his forehead with his handkerchief. "Let us send our prayers with Rise and lift our voices in song this evening to tell Satan that he cannot triumph as long as there is one soul willing to stand up to him. The human heart is chilled and the soul is challenged, and yet our God rolls on and comforts those who will follow. To Rise's family I extend my hand and the promise of a just God, who will heal the heavy heart and rest the weary soul. As you leave the church today, stop and pass a word to the mother who has lost her son and the grandparents who have lost a grandson. Comfort them and find comfort in your own fellowship and the love of a just God. Amen."

C.J. played and the choir sang softly. The sound of shuffling feet and people singing sounded farther away than usual. It had been the worst week of my life. Nothing that I believed in seemed to matter anymore. I had stopped crying outside, but I could still feel the tears falling inside. There weren't many people at the funeral, and the line to take a final look at Rise had soon finished. Dad put his arm around me when I started toward the front of the church.

The crying came again, and I had to clench my teeth to keep from making a noise. The weight in the middle of my chest made me feel as if I was sinking into myself, as if I might fall at any moment. When I got to the casket, I could barely see through the tears. He looked so small. So small and helpless in his dark suit and tie.

I'm sorry. I'm so sorry, Rise. I wish there was something I could do.

"You want to sit next to an old lady going out to the cemetery?" Miss Lassiter asked.

"I'm not going, ma'am," I said.

"That's all right, honey," she said. "That's just all right. I understand how hard it is."

When the last of the mourners had left St. Philip's, and it was only me and C.J. and Elder Smitty sitting in the church, C.J. started playing jazz. It wasn't hot jazz, but real soft, and sweet, and beautiful. From where I sat, I could see C.J.'s face lit by the light from over the music. His eyes were closed as he played, and I could imagine the thoughts flooding through him and into his fingers. Rise would have liked that. I knew when I died that's what I would want, C.J. sitting at the organ finding the right notes to send me away.

It wasn't just the tiredness, the deep-in-the-bone weariness that kept me sitting. It was the feeling of not knowing how to go on anymore, that all the things I had learned about living were wrong if all it led to was a few people sitting in the quiet of a church as the undertakers rolled the casket toward the side door and the waiting hearse. Mom came by, looking drawn, stray wisps of hair

in her face, her eyes red and puffy, and asked if I was coming home.

"I'd like to wait for C.J.," I told her.

She nodded and headed toward the back of the church, where Dad was waiting.

C.J. played longer than I thought he would, and I was almost dozing off when he stopped. He looked and saw me and Elder Smitty still sitting in the pews and came down.

"Boy, you can play that organ," Elder Smitty said. "You got a real gift. Keep it up."

"Thank you," C.J. said.

Outside on the steps they were just finished getting the cars organized, and the hearse was trying to get out into the afternoon traffic. Up the street a woman was struggling carrying packages and pulling a child along by the hand.

"She's probably got his new school clothes in those packages," C.J. said.

"Yeah, probably," I said.

My thoughts ran for a minute to Little Man. He would have been just starting high school. They hadn't had any trouble finding him. The paper said the police found him hiding on the roof of his house. I was glad to know they got him, but I was mad when they put in that he had been crying when they took him to jail, as if crying was something to be ashamed of doing.

Rise, my blood brother, was crying when he died. I had cried with him. And for him. Now I wanted to push it all away.

"Yo, you okay?" C.J. asked me.

"Yeah, I'm okay," I said.

"It's not the same anymore, right?" he asked. "When things like that happen to people you've been real tight with, it changes life."

"I don't know," I said. "I guess we just go on and see what happens. You okay?"

"If I tell you something—you'll try not to be mad?"

"Like what?"

"I'm real sorry that Rise is gone." C.J.'s voice lowered the way it does at times when he's serious. "But in a way, I'm glad we're not messing around with gangs and stuff anymore. That sounds wrong, I know."

"No, it don't, man. It's in the dark somewhere, but it's a feeling we got to have. And you're okay, man. Elder Smitty was right. You really do have a gift."

C.J. started telling me about how he had composed the tune blending Duke Ellington and some religious music from the nineteenth century. I really wasn't interested in all that, but he was so enthusiastic as we walked up the street, I didn't bother mentioning it. All the while I knew we were both thinking of Rise. And we were mourning. None of the sermons had eased the pain of his dying, or the mystery of his living.

I answered C.J. when he spoke, but in my mind, and in my heart, I was still talking to Rise, too. I was telling him that I would finish his life story, and I would make it as good as I could. And I would keep it forever, and maybe, just maybe, one day it would all make a perfect kind of sense.

As we walked, C.J. tried to push the conversation in a different direction, away from Rise. I could dig where he was coming from.

A tale of star-crossed love from Walter Dean Myers

The HERO

Here we see a busy school yard

Black, brown, and tan forms

Painting the illusion of music

With their bodies, ball-dancing between the

White lines of the court.

Young Damien Battle, comfortable in stride and gesture

Wearing his seventeen years easily around broad

Shoulders, saunters at the unhurried pace of

Hero knowing that the space that

Opens before him is his due.

Beside him, perhaps a half step

Behind, his friend Kevin chatters easily.

They are young and proud and Black

For them life is a ripe orange

Succulent and sweet, ready to be devoured

And here are Sledge and Chico

Rivals from the other side of the Avenue

Their tribe is the more familiar

We have seen them on every corner

Of every city in America. They make us walk

Faster. They make us think of locked doors.

Of differences we would like to deny.

Do Sledge's eyes meet Damien's?

Does he sneer as he spins his basketball

On one brown finger as if it was the World?

Does he speak?

Does he speak?

We listen as Sledge's mocking voice

Lifts itself above the background clatter

"Yo, Chico, check it out."

More gripping stories from
WALTER DEAN MYERS

Hc 0-06-029523-6
Pb 0-06-447288-4
Au 0-69-452535-9

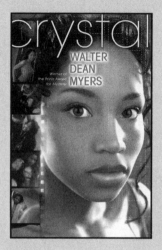

Pb 0-06-447312-0

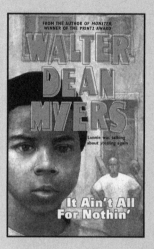

Pb 0-06-447311-2

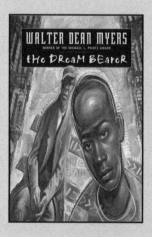

Hc 0-06-029521-X
Pb 0-06-447289-2
Au 0-06-054277-2

Hc 0-06-029146-X
Pb 0-06-440930-9
Au 0-06-008968-7

Hc 0-06-028077-8
Pb 0-06-440731-4

HarperTempest
An Imprint of HarperCollinsPublishers

Amistad
An Imprint of HarperCollinsPublishers

www.harperteen.com

More gripping stories from
WALTER DEAN MYERS

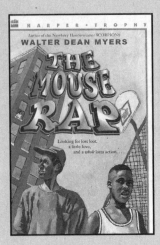

Pb 0-06-440356-4

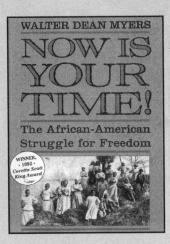

Pb 0-06-446120-3

Pb 0-06-440462-5

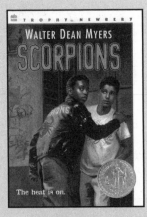

Hc 0-06-024364-3
Pb 0-06-440623-7

Hc 0-06-029519-8
Pb 0-06-447290-6
Au 0-06-074765-X